GRIZZLY

CAUTIONARY TALES FOR LOVERS OF SQUEAM

BLUBBERS
AND
SICKSTERS

WARNING!

IF YOU LOVE YOUR BROTHERS AND SISTERS
READ NO FURTHER!

WHERE ARE YOU GOING?
STOP! UNLESS YOU ARE AN ONLY CHILD ...
IN WHICH CASE YOU MAY CARRY ON,
BECAUSE NOBODY WILL MISS YOU.

GRIZZLY TALES

'CAUTIONARY TALES FOR LOVERS' OF SQUEAM'

BLUBBERS AND SICKSTERS

JAMIE RIX

Illustrated by Steven Pattison

WARNING!

IF YOU READ ANY FURTHER YOU WILL UPSET YOUR
BROTHERS AND SISTERS WHEN YOU DISAPPEAR
INTO THE DARKNESS AND DON'T COME BACK ... OR
DO COME BACK IN SIXTY-THREE JIFFY BAGS.

Orion
Children's Books

Ignore that £10 note. It's been put there to tempt you into The Darkness.
There is something evil holding on to the other end of that £10 note and you do NOT want to meet it!

For Jonty and Caroline

First published in Great Britain in 2008
by Orion Children's Books
a division of the Orion Publishing Group Ltd
Orion House
5 Upper St Martin's Lane
London WC2H 9EA
An Hachette Livre company

Greed will be the death of you!

Cut out the following poem and carry it with you while you are reading this book. It will serve to remind you that in The Hothell Darkness you must always be on your guard! Plus, you can cover your head with the piece of paper should it happen to rain frogs.

<u>GREEDY GUTS</u>

WHATEVER GREEDY SEES HE ALWAYS WANTS
WHATEVER GREEDY WANTS HE ALWAYS TAKES
WHATEVER GREEDY HAS HE ALWAYS WISHES
THAT BEFORE HE'D SNATCHED IT HE HAD HIT THE BRAKES.

BUT THAT'S NOT HOW A KIDDIE'S COOKIE CRUMBLES
WHEN INTO THIS HOT-HELL A KIDDIE STUMBLES . . .

NOW THAT HE HAS POCKETED A TENNER,
GREEDY GUTS HAS SOLD HIS TAINTED SOUL
TO A MAN WHO NEEDS NO SECOND INVITATION
TO BURY GREEDY IN A FIVE-STAR HOLE!

Cut out the following item as well, and use it as a hide-behind in the event of scary meltdown.

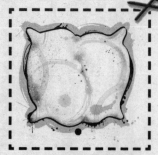

Welcome to
The Hothell Darkness

Breakfast 7.30am - 9.30am.
(No silly family squabbles unless by prior arrangement with the management)

In the event of a fire alarm stay exactly where you are. There are no fire exits, so what would be the point of running around like a headless chicken when you're going to burn anyway? Talking of headless chickens, please avoid sacrificing poultry in your room unless you have received the required permissions from the Hothell Witch Doctor. His surgery is open between 11.00 - 13.00 for snake-related revenges and 15.00 - 17.00 for head-shrinkings, voodoo dolls and general cursings. Monkey-cooking lessons available on request.

The Night-night Porter

Hello again.

You look more like a bad penny every time you turn up. Your room's still ready. Only this time. because you're such a frequent visitor. I've upgraded you and put you in the tiniest room in the hothell. the Youngest Child's Room. or as our guests prefer to call it. the Pent-up Suite. Very small. Very stressful. You get to sleep in a cardboard box. have uninterrupted views over a brick wall and enjoy the constant company of the incontinent hothell cat. If you start to go a little stir-crazy. there are plenty of games to play. Notching the bedpost is one. swinging the cat around your head is another. although there may not be quite enough room and you may end up creating a piece of modern art on the walls . . .

Talking of splattered brains. how's your behaviour these days? I need to check that you haven't turned goody-goody since I saw you last. Only the baddest children make it into the Hothell Darkness! And I tend to find that the baddest children are blubbers and sicksters. No love lost there.

OF COURSE you know who I mean . . . blubbers blub to get their sicksters into trouble. prefer fighting to talking and make the room smell like a barn when they remove their trainers. Sicksters make blubbers sick with all their giggling and crying and chattering on the phone. and they only have to see a shop to wet themselves! Maybe you know them better as brothers and sisters.

So let's see how bad you are . . .

ANSWER TRUTHFULLY!

1) When your sickster lies in the bath for hours, have you ever lobbed an electric fire into the water and shouted 'Catch!'?

2) When your little blubber is angry with you and punches you with all his might, do you laugh and ask if there is a butterfly in the room that has just brushed you with its wings?

3) When you feel car sick do you wind down the window and vomit onto the road or shut the window, lock the door and turn to face your blubbers and sicksters?

4) When there is one crumpet left on the plate and you know that crumpets are your blubber's favourite food, do you cry 'Whoops!' and 'accidentally' knock the crumpet into the cat litter tray?

5) Prior to a match, have you ever stuck a picture of your sickster's face onto a dartboard?

If you've answered **YES** to all of these questions you are a normal blubber or sickster, but an evil individual. Therefore, you are most welcome in the Hothell Darkness. I have taken the liberty of having your bags taken up to your room and booked you a table for dinner in the Lizard Lounge. You'll be served up on Table 29 and eaten by a large lizard called Mr Dewsberry.

I was a blubber once and VERY good I was too! I've never forgot those skills I learned at my mother's knee. At the time I was under the table attaching a bomb to her shoelaces, because she wouldn't let me have a second banana milkshake.

It was from my time as a blubber that I developed my lifelong hatred of children. Not just one or two either, pretty much all of them. It was a very shocking incident that still pains me to recall. My lifelong hatred of children stems from the time my cruel sickster told me she could see my pants sticking out the bottom of my shorts and everyone at school heartlessly called me 'Longpants'! Being a sensitive blubber, I blubbed long and hard to get my sickster and all her mates into trouble. I blubbed for a week, but it didn't work. At the end of that week I decided that never again would I be a blubber and became an Evil Mastermind instead with a festering brainbox that was brilliant for thinking up nasty revenges.

But I digress. We're not here to talk about me. We're here to lock YOU up for ever and cause you some not inconsiderable pain. In between tortures you might find yourself tempted to dwell on the hopelessness and futility of your situation. Don't be silly. Take your mind off it by reading about the misfortunes of our OTHER guests in our Visitor's

Book (or as I prefer to call it The Book of Grizzly Tales). You'll have much more fun dwelling on the hopelessness and futility of THEIR situations instead!

The naughty children in these tales are all blubbers and sicksters, so you can expect some pretty brutal stuff: one-on-one cricket battering, hours of ruined hellwork, milk showers, an ooze cruise, a barracuda bikini challenge, a pair of peeled eyeballs, three half-mice and a chair with a secret steel spike under the cushion! And that's just what they can expect when they get down here!

It was only a joke!

Please Look in the Mirror!

Slow down!

Don't trim me again!

Liquidate the plumber!

No Good Ever Comes of Wart!

Now they've started shouting. Why do I always get the noisy bickering ones? It's like living in a railway carriage with sixty-five million iPod users! Why can't I get the silent sort you get in church? You know. HOLY blubbers and sicksters. living in Monastries. the ones who take a VOW OF SILENCE.

Our first tale is a tale of big sickster versus little sickster. We all think of BLUBBERS as the vicious ones. but when you realise that black widow spiders are GIRLS. it makes you think again. Anyway this was a horribly one-sided contest. In the red corner. a vicious old trout called Dorothy May. In the blue corner. her little sickster — a tiddly sprat called Pettie. They are the Piranha Sisters. And we all know how deadly piranhas can be!

The Night-flight Porter

THE PIRANHA SISTERS

It all began with an April Fool that Petie fell for hook, line and sinker. It was 06.30 am on April 1st, when Dorothy May ran into her little sister's bedroom and woke her with a start.

'Petie! Wake up! There's a tiger on the lawn!'

'Where?' mewed Petie, opening her eyes to instant angst.

'On the lawn.'

'No. I mean I can't see it.' Petie had scanned the lawn and found it wanting for tigers. But Dorothy May had an explanation for that.

'Tigers didn't get to the top of the food chain by being seen, Petie. They're the best at killing because they're invisible. If you could see it, it wouldn't be a tiger, would it?' Part of the problem was that Petie believed everything her big sister said. Petie was kind, you see, and thought everyone else was kind too. She didn't realise that some people (and that included her big sister) were born liars and out to do her harm.

Did someone call me?

'Oh, help!' shrieked Petie. 'We're all going to be eaten in our beds.'

'Yes, I rather think we are!' Dorothy May grinned.

Petie panicked. 'Run, Dorothy May! Run!'

'You run, Petie. I'll wait here and save you.'

'You'd do that for me?' gasped Petie.

'You are my little sister.' Dorothy May smiled like a slippery snake.

'Oh, you're the best big sister a girl could ever have!' wept Petie. 'I love you.' Then she ran out of the bedroom with only one thought on her mind: to get away from the tigers. In fact, she ran straight into the street, caught the next bus to Scotland and went missing for three days, until the police found her and took her to see experts to convince her that there really were no tigers in England.

'But these aren't experts,' said Petie softly. 'This is

a zoo. These are zebras. What do they know about tigers?'

'They'd know if there were any loose ones about,' said the policeman. 'Trust me.'

* * *

From that day on, big sister had little sister firmly in her grip. Once Dorothy May realised that Petie was gullible, every day was joker-day. Pranks became part of the daily torture. She bent a long nail around her index finger and told Petie it had gone right through the bone.

'If you don't believe me,' she said, 'listen.' Then she screamed with pain until Petie joined in.

She sat in the bath with an axe through her head.

'That's plastic,' said Petie. 'You wouldn't be alive if you had a real axe through your brain.'

'Think what you like,' whispered Dorothy May in her best Poor-Me-I'm-Dying voice, 'but this blood's not ketchup!' It *was* in fact.

That was Dorothy May's bold double bluff. 'Taste it if you don't believe me,' she said, holding out a palmful of red goo for Petie to lick. Her little sister didn't stop wailing for nine hundred minutes.

Dorothy May even pretended to poke her eyeballs out on a gooseberry bush, before staggering towards Petie with zombie arms.

'Petie!' she groaned. 'I can't see. I'm holding my eyes in my hands. Help me push them back in.' Then she pretended to slip – 'Whoops!' – and crushed her fleshy eyeballs on a patio paving slab.

'Aaaaaaagh!' screamed Petie.

'Grapes,' sniggered Dorothy May, as Petie scooted away from the blinding as fast as a scalded cheetah.

Not all of Dorothy May's jokes were gross; however, a large number were designed to get Petie into trouble. Like the 'acid alien' story.

'Aliens!' gasped the younger girl at breakfast that day.

'Oh yes. Earth is being invaded by alien monsters that shoot acid from their fingers!' Watching Petie swallow her lies gave Dorothy May even more pleasure than the time she gate-crashed Petie's Horse and Rider birthday party and forced all of Petie's friends to play a game of 'Pin The Tail on Petie'.

'Acid from their fingers?' gasped Petie. '*Real* acid?!'

'Oh yes! And they look like teachers,' added Dorothy May, lowering her voice in case any aliens were eavesdropping. 'That's their cunning disguise.' This meant, of course, that Petie, later that day, gathered her friends together in the playground and issued a Code Red Warning.

'They're everywhere!' she squeaked. 'I know you think they're teachers but they're not.'

'Look out!' squealed a bespectacled mouse called Margot. 'They're coming!' Two teachers were strolling over to see what the girl-gathering was about.

'Quick!' panicked Petie. 'Save yourselves! Run for your lives! Cover your eyes so the acid can't burn you!'

'What's going on?' asked one of the teachers.

'Don't listen to her honeyed words!' yelled Petie. 'They'll try to get you back into the classroom, but it's a trick. Run! Run like the wind! Run home and never come back!' Petie's words started a stampede of screaming children, and put both teachers in hospital with broken bones. The next day poor Petie was suspended and a black mark set against her name in the Behaviour Book.

Dorothy May never said sorry.

But later that same night, as the carriage clock chimed midnight, Dorothy May woke up to find that she was not alone. Her window had blown open and a cold, whistling wind was shrieking her name.

'Dorothy May! Dorothy May!'

Dorothy May sat up sharply, just as a skeleton materialised at the end of her bed. It hovered above her bedclothes with bones that glowed green and a lower jaw that dislocated and dropped open every time it spoke. 'The practical jokes must end,' it said. 'Stop tormenting your little sister or the jokes will turn on you.'

Most children would have been terrified, but not Dorothy May.

'Says who, bony? For all I know you're one of Petie's jokes.'

Then she threw her pillow at the skeleton, expecting to knock it off the fishing line from which it was suspended, but the pillow passed straight through its ribcage. There was no line. The skeleton was real.

'Ignore my warning at your peril,' it said. 'If you

do not stop *I* will happen.' Dorothy May snorted.

'*You* will happen! What does that mean? I suggest you practise your English before failing to scare me again!'

'*I* will happen!'

'Oh, I get it! A skeleton will happen. So Petie's going to turn into a skeleton, is she?' But the skeleton did not reply and faded away. 'Or is it me? Hello,' called out Dorothy May. 'Hello. Tch, stupid!'

* * *

The next day was Petie's birthday. A big day was planned. A school trip to the Houses of Parliament, a visit to see granny in her Old Folk's Home and a much longed-for birthday party at the swimming pool. Petie had been planning it for weeks. But then so had Dorothy May!

At five o'clock in the morning, she climbed out of her bedroom window and took the early train up to London. Then she applied her grey make-up behind a bush, unwrapped the old paraffin lamp that she'd found in the garage, and was in position in Parliament Square when Petie and her class arrived.

They were marching up the pavement in crocodile file, admiring the statues of Britain's great and good, when the statue of Florence Nightingale leaped down off her pedestal and landed in front of them with a gut-wrenching groan. Petie and her school-friends thought the statue had come to life. They jumped out of their skins, screamed and scattered like frightened pigeons, and allowed Dorothy May to slip away unnoticed.

She had just washed off her make-up in the Serpentine and was strolling through Hyde Park on the way to the station to catch a train home, when a cry caught her attention. 'Look out!'

From nowhere the statue of a cavalry officer on a horse crashed onto the pavement in front of her. The officer's lance missed her head by inches.

'Sorry, love. Are you all right?' The voice belonged to the driver of a crane who had been lowering the statue onto its plinth when the cable had snapped.

'I'm fine,' mumbled Dorothy May, but she wasn't. She was spooked that her own prank had suddenly become real and inside her head she couldn't stop hearing the voice of the skeleton; 'or the jokes will turn on you.'

* * *

It didn't stop her from getting on that train, though. Nor from putting on a long black cape and hoodie, swapping her lamp for a garden scythe and visiting the Old Folk's home dressed as Death.

'Hello,' she said in as deep a voice as she could muster. 'I've come to see Granny Piranha.' The nurse who had opened the door took one look at this sinister figure dressed in black, apparently with no face, because it was hidden inside the hood, and collapsed onto the floor. Dorothy May stepped over her body and walked upstairs to see her granny. On the way she passed the Day Room, a bright and sunny room where the elderly residents sat and chatted over a nice cup of tea. Imagine their horror when who should put his head around the door, but Death!

'Morning. Morning. Catch up with you all later.' What followed was a mass faint and kicking in of pacemakers. When she opened the door of her granny's room, therefore, she knew what reaction to expect.

'Aaaagh!' That was granny. 'Has my time come?' For Petie, who was playing draughts with her granny, the shock was unbearable. She burst into hysterical tears, thinking that her granny was going to die there and then in front of her! All the more shocking, therefore, when Death started laughing and ran away.

It was only a joke!

Excuses won't save you now. Dorothy May!

A few seconds later, having slipped through the fire exit into the car park, Dorothy May was removing her cape when she bumped into the real thing. At least he said he was the real thing.

'I am Death,' boomed the tall cowled figure in front of her. 'How's about you and I pull up a tombstone and get acquainted?'

Dorothy May was so terrified that her eyeballs bulged in her head, and for the first time in her life she feared for it. Luckily Death was arrested for wearing a hoodie in a built-up area and whisked away in a Black Maria, but it set those voices ringing in her head again, 'Or the jokes will turn on you.'

* * *

And so to late afternoon, and Dorothy May's

fiendish finalé. She arrived at the swimming pool with a bulging beach bag and was waved through by the attendant. Instead of going to change, however, she took a detour, broke into the filter room underneath the pool and hid the clockwork submarines (that she'd spent hours painting) inside the pool filter. All she had to do now was wait for Petie and her friends to jump into the water and her Master Prank would be revealed! She didn't have to wait long.

Ten minutes later, the pool was full of joyful shrieks and laughter when Dorothy May cranked open the valve through which water flowed into the pool, and released her shoal of terror.

'Look!' shouted one of the lifeguards, rising in his seat and pointing at a large shadow in the deep end. 'There's something in the water!'

Petie looked down and screamed. 'It's piranha!'

'Everybody out! Everybody out!' screamed the lifeguard, causing instant and uncontrollable panic. Children yelled and flapped and fought their way to the edge of the pool where their parents plucked them from the water. Meanwhile, down in the bowels of the leisure

23

centre, through a ventilation grille, Dorothy May was watching Petie scream.

'Mummy! Save me from the piranha!'

How Dorothy May laughed. It was quite the most brilliant practical joke she had ever played. In fact she was so pleased with herself that she sang Happy Birthday to Petie, punctuated by snorts of derision . . .

'Happy Birthday to you,
I made a piranha-present for you,
Painted subs red and yellow,
Scared the pants off you too!'

Little did she know that she was singing to herself!

It was only a joke!

As was what followed, Dorothy May. As is what happens to you in this hothell on a daily basis. It's all just ONE GREAT BIG LAUGH! Such a shame you can't see the FUNNY side!

Later that night, when Dorothy May stepped into her bath, the words of the midnight skeleton could not have been further from her mind. But when, suddenly, her bathwater drained back up the taps and her bath refilled with water that contained clockwork submarines crudely painted to look like piranha, she could think of nothing else. In fact, she was just thinking that she should get out of the bath when the clockwork toys transformed into the *real* thing.

Piranha by name, piranha by nature! The little fish, individually no bigger than a bar of soap, attacked en masse with their jutting lower jaws and serrated teeth. They latched onto her flesh with such speed that she didn't even have time to scream.

Less than a minute later, when the blood-red water had stopped boiling, there was nothing left of Dorothy May, except a few white bones – the same bones in fact that had tried to warn her of her fate the night before.

'If you do not stop,' the ghostly skeleton had said, '*I* will happen.'

She's down here now – or rather, her bones are.

I thought about hanging her in the dining room as a warning to guests who won't eat their food. You know the sort of thing: this is what you can expect to look like if you refuse to eat Worm Pie! But diners were using her ribs to stack their trays. So I tried her out in the Games Room, using her long leg bones as snooker cues, but players kept putting the bones back in the wrong place and her skeleton started changing shape until it looked like a badger. So now I just mess with her head and use her skull as a football.

Sadly I've never had the company of Petie. Released from her torturer, the little sickster grew into a strong, independent woman with a lingering fear of baths. A few years ago, when she wrote her autobiography, she put her phobia down to finding a skeleton in the bath on her ninth birthday. She wrote . . .

It was I who found Dorothy May's body. My nine-year-old screams brought my parents rushing upstairs.

'What is it?' they shouted. 'What's happened, Petie?' So I showed them. And the strange thing was that when they saw the grinning skeleton in the bath they burst out laughing.

'It's another one of Dorothy May's jokes,' roared my father. 'I'll put it in the bin.' And that's exactly what he did. He threw my big sister away!

Which means, of course, that I, little Petie, most definitely had the last laugh. And I think I rather deserved it... don't you?

I do! What I'm going to tell you now is NOT a joke, because it's about a special time of year when I get my biggest intake of blubbers and sicksters. I'll give you a clue when it is. It's a time of great celebration. For ME, obviously, not you lot. For YOU kiddies it's the END of the world!

Please Look in the Mirror!

Fick knows what I'm talking about.

Any ideas when it is? It's New Year, of course! That time of year when stupid little children make promises they can't keep. And when they can't keep them, that means they're bad, and when they're bad, they're MINE!

It was only a joke!

Please Look in the Mirror!
Slow down!

Don't trim me again!

Liquidate the plumber!

No Good Ever Comes of Wart!

THE CRYSTAL EYE

Once upon a New Year, there lived a gypsy woman with only one good eye. The other eye was dead. It scratched around in a dried-out socket and swirled with milky clouds. The truth was it wasn't an eye at all. It was a crystal ball, through which she watched the wicked world and spotted selfish children who most deserved her attention.

* * *

The Finnegan twins were not *all* bad. Half of them was good. Although it was impossible to tell them apart by sight, it was easy when you got to know them. Finn was always an angel, while Fick was never less than a devil! He hated being an identical twin, because people always thought of him and his brother as *one* person. This was bad news at Christmas, because it meant that

29

Fick and Finn were always given presents to share. Finn never minded. He liked playing games with his brother. But Fick hated sharing. His idea of a good game was a competition with Finn to see who owned the most toys. It stood to reason, therefore, that far from being a bundle of festive fun and frolics, Christmas in the Finnegan family was a time of war and stress.

On this particular Christmas, the day got off to a bad start when Fick ignored the labels on the presents under the tree ...

For Fick and Finn
Love
Mummy and Daddy
X

... and opened all of them before Fick had even got up. Then, by citing the little-known motto of *'Openers keepers! Non-Openers Weepers!'*, he justified keeping every present for himself, and locked his booty into the steel cage that he'd built to keep his toys away from his brother. FICK'S PRESENTS! said the sign on the gate. DEATH TO ANYONE WHO EVEN THINKS ABOUT LOOKING AT THEM!

The rest of the family came downstairs at the normal time to find Fick kissing the presents through the bars of the cage.

'Oh, I do love Christmas!' he sighed happily as he rolled onto his back and saw his family staring down at him. 'Oh hello, everyone. Happy Christmas.' But nobody replied and Finn's bottom lip was trembling.

'What's the matter now?' snapped Fick. 'You're not going to cry all day, are you, Finn? Christmas is supposed to be fun!'

'I thought half of those presents were mine,' said Finn.

'They were,' said Fick, 'but now they're not. In the words spoken by the innkeeper to Mary and Joseph when he bunged them in a stable, "Get used to it!" But when Mrs Finnegan waded in on Finn's side, Fick flew off the handle.

'I *hate* being a twin!' he screamed. 'I don't want to own my presents with Finn. I want them for *me*!'

'You really must learn to share, Fick,' said Mr Finnegan wearily.

If Mr and Mrs Finnegan had been given a crocodile every time they'd said, 'You really must learn to share, Fick,' they'd have been crocodile farmers by now!

'Maybe that could be your New Year Resolution,' proposed Mrs Finnegan, 'learning to share.'

At this suggestion Fick erupted with rage. 'I've got a better idea!' he seethed. 'Let's sort out this present problem *now*!'

'On Christmas Day?' she protested. 'Can't it wait?'

'Oh yes, let's just put my happiness on hold, why don't we!' howled Fick. 'No, it can't wait! You want me to share with Finn then LET'S DO IT!' When Fick's voice shook the bars in the hamster's cage it was time to do as he said.

Fick piled all of the Christmas presents into a wheelbarrow and plunged onto the snowy streets with Finn and Mr Finnegan running to keep up.

'Where are we going?' his father complained.

'You'll see soon enough,' said Fick. 'Ooh, look!' They were passing a department store window. Fick stopped and pointed at the glittering gifts inside. 'That's what I want for next Christmas!' he said greedily.

'What exactly are you pointing at?' asked Mr Finnegan.

'I'm not exactly pointing at anything!' sneered Fick. 'I want the whole shop. Come on.'

* * *

They arrived at the sawmill where Mr Finnegan worked. Having unlocked the factory door with his father's key, Fick switched on the circular saw and tossed a skateboard onto the conveyor belt.

'IF YOU WANT TO SHARE THEN WE'LL SHARE!' he bellowed petulantly over the screech of the spinning blade.

'WHAT ARE YOU DOING?' hollered his father. The skateboard had been sucked in whole and spat out in two pieces.

'THIS WAY, WE OWN HALF EACH!' sneered Fick. 'IT'S WHAT YOU WANTED.'

'DON'T BE SO CHILDISH,' screamed his father.

'BUT I *AM* A CHILD,' jeered Fick, and to prove it he chucked another armful of toys onto the belt. The metal teeth bit and burned, flinging out two halves of a football, two halves of a Robomorph, two halves of a Gamepod, two halves of a tortoise . . .

'NO!' screamed Finn, grabbing the tortoise from the shadow of the blade. 'YOU CAN'T SHOVE A LIVING ANIMAL THROUGH A SAW!'

Actually, you can. You just can't TELL anyone about it.

'MAKE UP YOUR MIND!' jeered Fick. 'DO YOU OR DO YOU NOT WANT TO SHARE OUR PRESENTS?'

'*YOU* CAN HAVE THE TORTOISE,' shouted Finn.

'NO, DON'T BOTHER,' grumbled Fick. 'I'll CUT UP *THIS* INSTEAD.' And he sliced his father's wheelbarrow straight down the middle.

As he did so an all-seeing crystal eye swivelled and scraped in its dried-out socket.

* * *

That night, at Christmas dinner, when Fick pulled a cracker with his mother, a Romany Fortune

Horse fell out of the cardboard tube with instructions to MAKE A WISH. Fick leaned forward to grab it but his mother beat him to it.

'My turn,' she smiled, closing her fingers around the horse and shutting her eyes. 'I wish that Fick was as good as Finn!'

The horse whinnied as the old woman reined in its head. Then the wooden wheels of her caravan turned across the rutted path and headed back down the track.

* * *

Meanwhile, Fick was throwing another tantrum.

'You hate me!' he shrieked. 'You're always wishing I was a goody-goody like Finn. Well, I'm not! In fact, from now on, I'm going to be twice as bad!' And he stormed upstairs to his bedroom with a face as long a gargoyle's shadow.

'Come back here now!' Mr Finnegan shouted after him. 'Or you'll ruin Christmas for everyone!' Far from being ruined, however, the rest of Christmas was an altogether more pleasant affair with Fick barricaded into his bedroom.

* * *

He was still there five days later. Come New Year's

Eve, Fick was sulking upstairs when the doorbell rang. Finn was downstairs making his New Year Resolutions.

'To do more cleaning, tidy my room, not drop litter . . .' He put down his pen and went to open the door.

'Are you Fick?' asked the old gypsy woman on the doorstep. She wore rainbow-coloured skirts and jangled with silver jewellery.

'No,' said Finn. 'I'm Finn.'

She tugged the clump of hairs on her chin and spat at his feet. The white gob frothed and boiled on the toe of Finn's shoe.

'I hate twins!' she muttered. 'Go get your brother!' As Finn ran upstairs, she pulled a large gold-framed mirror from behind her back and leant it up against the door jamb. Strangely there was no reflection. The glass was full of smoke.

It took ten minutes to persuade Fick to come out of his bedroom. Only when Finn explained that there was a lady downstairs with a present for him did he rush to the front door. The old woman grasped Fick's wrist and tugged him close. Her breath smelled like fetid flower water.

'This mirror belongs to you,' she said.

'You mean it's mine to keep *for ever*?' he asked bluntly.

'For as long as it is needed.'

'So it's not Finn's?'

'Is that all you care about?' dribbled the gypsy woman, plucking out her crystal eye and polishing it on her patched velvet collar.

'No,' he said cheekily. 'I care about *this* too: why haven't I got a reflection? I'm not a vampire!' Fick didn't trust a looking glass that wouldn't let him look.

 'You will see what the rest of the world sees soon enough,' she cackled. 'But do not wish your reflection in the glass, Fick, for once inside, it can never leave.'

'Is this like one of those jokes off the telly?' he said. 'Is there a man with a camera hiding behind that bush?'

'No,' she hissed. 'This is your last chance to make amends. New Year is a time to embrace what is new and discard what you no longer want.'

'A mirror can't help me do that,' he scoffed.

'*This* mirror can,' said the crone with the crooked smile.

> *Slow down!*

That's just Cat moaning. Ignore her. She always gets a headache at this time of day . . . when the traffic builds up at rush hour.

* * *

Finn was locked out of Fick's bedroom while Mr Finnegan hung the mirror on the wall.

'It's *my* mirror,' Fick had told his twin. 'You're not allowed to look.' When the mirror was up, Fick ran his eye along the gilded frame to see if he could spot where the smoke was getting in. Instead of a hole however, he found an inscription, which said: LEX TALIONIS.

'What does that mean?' he asked his father.

'It's Latin,' said Mr Finnegan. 'It means "like for like".'

'And what does *that* mean?'

His father shrugged. 'It means replacing one thing with something identical, I guess.'

'And what does *that* mean?'

'I don't know,' said his father.

'Well, you're not very well informed, are you?' said Fick. Then he added rudely, 'You can go now. Shut the door on your way out.'

Once Fick was alone, the smoke inexplicably dispersed.

'Ooh spooky!' he mocked as his reflection appeared in the glass. To prove that he was not afraid, he stuck out his tongue and said sarcastically, 'I'm really scared of you.'

'And so you should be!' replied his reflection.

Fick froze with his mouth open. 'No,' he said softly. 'That's wrong. Reflections can't talk. You can't do anything that *I* don't do first.'

'Really?' it laughed. 'Then how come I can do this?' And in the mirror it ran up the wall, stood upside-down on the ceiling and scratched its head.

'But you're my slave!' gawped Fick, who hadn't moved. 'You do what *I* tell you!' The reflection dropped to the floor.

'Not me,' it said, 'because I'm not a normal reflection. I'm the reflection you don't want to see.'

'Then I'll shut my eyes,' said the boy, defiantly.

'That doesn't work, I'm afraid. Now that I'm here, here I shall stay, unless . . .' The hairs on the back of Fick's neck stood on end.

'Unless what?'

'Unless someone comes in here to take my place.' From the way his reflection was grinning, Fick had a horrible feeling that the 'someone' in question was him.

It was!

Suddenly, in the mirror, he saw the bedroom door burst open. A dozen festering zombies staggered into the room. Their dead-white faces wailed and groaned like souls in torture, their clothes hung in rags, their useless limbs dangled from thin strips of skin, their eyes swung from shredded nerves, their scabby heads swirled with flies and their putrid flesh ruptured with fat, wriggling maggots.

Sounds like a Boy Band I know!

Fick swung round, expecting to see these hellish creatures behind him, but the bedroom was empty. That could only mean one thing . . . Slowly, his breath held tight, Fick turned back to the mirror, but the zombies had gone, leaving in their wake a faint after-whiff of decay and boredom.

'Did you smell them?' laughed his reflection. 'That's the wonder of this mirror. It can interlace realities.'

'Were they dead?' asked Fick.

'Dead*ish*,' came the jaunty reply. 'They'll never get any deader.'

'So who are they?'

'Children,' said the reflection. '*Bad* children. Selfish little siblings who refuse to get on with their brothers and sisters.'

'This is all about Christmas, isn't it?' said Fick aggressively. 'Just because I've kept more presents than Finn you're going to turn me into a zombie!'

'I'm saying that should you ever be unlucky enough to find yourself inside this mirror, that's what you'll look like!' said the reflection.

'Then I'll just have to stay *out* of the mirror, won't I?' sneered Fick.

'That,' it replied, 'is easier said than done! You'll have to love your brother, stop fighting, share your toys. Can you do that? Not just today, but for the rest of your life?' Fick snorted.

'For the rest of my life?' he said. 'Without even one day off? No. I don't think so.'

* * *

The crystal eye had seen into the future and *knew* that this would be his answer.

Without warning, Fick's reflection started to melt. Its bottom jaw clattered to the floor leaving its tongue and throat exposed, its eyes bulged and popped out of its skull, and its skin split as a thrashing ball of worms burst through its flesh.

'Come and join us!' thundered the dead-eyed zombie in the mirror.

'What are you?' shouted Fick.

'A future *you*!' came the terrifying reply.

'You're not me,' yelled the boy. 'You're bad gypsy magic! I'm *never* joining you in there!' Cockroaches scuttled out of its mouth as Fick's rotting reflection threw back its head and laughed.

'Then so be it!' it roared. 'We'll just have to come out and get you!' In the mirror, the bedroom door burst open again and the flaky flesh of the zombie tribe re-entered. This time they were chanting, 'Pick up Fick! Quickity Quick! Pick up Fick! Quickity Quick!'

'GO AWAY!' screamed Fick, grabbing his bedside lamp and hurling it at the mirror. The glass shattered into a thousand pieces, exploding the zombies into oblivion.

Grabbing the chance to escape, Fick rushed across his empty bedroom, wrenched open the door and ran downstairs into the non-zombie arms of his family. He was just in time to turn over a new leaf. With only seconds left till midnight, Fick made his New Year resolution.

'I *will* be good like Finn,' he said. 'I'll share everything I've got. I promise that from now on you're going to see a new me!' It was generally acknowledged by everyone that they were rather looking forward to that!

* * *

For the first few days Fick tried really hard to be nice to his brother. He bit his tongue when Finn finished the tomato ketchup. He held back a scream when Finn was bought a new pair of trainers. He put his fist in his pocket when Finn ordered the same ice cream as him in a restaurant. He even played boring snakes and ladders when Finn asked him to. But when Finn went into Fick's room and switched on his computer to play 'Flesh of the Living Dead', Fick saw red and decked his twin brother with a right hook.

'That's mine!' he screamed like a three-year-old. 'Get your greasy mitts off my keyboard!' In one fell swoop, his New Year resolution was in tatters. Fick chucked his brother out of his bedroom and slammed the door, only noticing *then* that the mirror was no longer in pieces on the floor.

* * *

When Fick saw that the mirror had reassembled itself, he was nervous. When his reflection disappeared, he was scared. But when the old gypsy woman appeared in the glass, he was heart-stoppingly terrified!

'The time has come for me to take back what is mine,' she said.

'If you mean the mirror, you can have it!' whispered Fick. 'I don't want it.'

'It's not as simple as that.' She smiled. 'Now that you have met your reflection only one of you can stay.'

'Stay?'

'In the mirror,' she explained.

Fick tried to pretend that her threat didn't bother him, but his mouth was dry and the words stuck in his throat. 'Well, it's not going to be me,' he squeaked. 'I live out here, remember?'

'Not for much longer,' she said mysteriously.

in a trice, the gypsy woman turned back into Fick's reflection and leaped out of the mirror into the bedroom.

'What are you?' peeped the boy as his reflection stepped across the carpet towards him.

'Your better half,' grinned the boy's unnatural twin.

At that moment, Fick knew exactly what was going to happen to him.

'I'll be good!' he cried. 'I'll never be selfish again! I'll love Finn forever!'

'Too late!' smiled his reflection. Then it grabbed Fick by the throat and threw him through the glass.

* * *

It was cold inside the mirror. It smelled musty, like damp earth in a coffin. Fick was peering into his own bedroom, from where his smug reflection was now waving.

'Let me out!' shouted the boy behind the glass.

'Impossible!' said his reflection. 'We've changed places, Fick. I am a boy and you are my mirrored-slave.'

But Fick refused to believe him and took several

steps backwards. 'If you can jump out of the mirror so can I!' he shouted defiantly. He ran towards the back of the glass and leapt … but there was no way through. He cracked his head and knocked himself onto the floor.

'You're in there for good,' laughed Fick's reflection. 'You and every other selfish sibling!'

As the skin on the tips of Fick's fingers split and turned white, the door to the bedroom suddenly opened and Finn walked in.

Inside the mirror, Fick leaped to his feet and banged on the glass. 'Finn,' he hollered. 'Look in the mirror! Save me!'

But Finn was not looking at the mirror. He was staring at his twin brother in astonishment. For the first time in his life, Fick had just hugged him.

'I owe you an apology, Finn. I've been horrid to you all my life when we should have been friends. We should have been sharing stuff not fighting. It's my fault, and I want to put it right. I want my brother back.'

Finn asked if Fick had a fever. 'Not any more,' said the reflection. 'From now on, we share everything straight down the middle.'

'Noooooooooo!' cried the soon-to-be-zombie

trapped behind the glass. 'Look in here!' And that, as the tongue fell out of his mouth, was the last anyone ever heard from Fick.

It's true. He hasn't said a word since I brought him and his mirror down here into The Darkness. He blows on the back of the glass and writes messages in the condensation. but he hasn't worked out that he has to write in reverse yet. His last message looked like this.

why does nobody try to understand what I say?

Nobody understood what he was trying to say. I've put him over the sink in the Boys' Loo. You should see how terrified the boys are when they see a zombie's face looking back at them from the mirror. They think it's THEIR face! It's hysterical.

By the way. I've got a warning for all blubbers and sicksters.

BEWARE THE CRYSTAL EYE!

47

Do yourself a favour. Tonight and every night when you run upstairs to bed, check all the mirrors in the house — just in case your reflection ISN'T THERE! And listen out for any mysterious schitch-scratchings when it's dark. Then at least you'll know in advance if the old gypsy woman has got her one bad eye on you!

Talking of eyes . . . next time you're driving on a motorway keep your eyes PEELED for CROWS. You'll see them huddled in gangs by the side of the road, hopping from one foot to the other, wiping their beaks on their bottoms and haughtily eyeing the cars as they flash past, as if to say, 'Get off my dining table.' Occasionally one bird will hop lazily into the path of the oncoming traffic to peel a shrew off the tarmac or tug at the intestines of a squashed fox. It is a dangerous way to dine, yet weirdly the crows are never hit. By some sixth sense they know when cars are about to splatter them and they take off at the very last minute trailing carrion from their beaks. If you think I'm making this up, study the road kill at the side of the road. You can travel from Land's End to John O'Groats and you will NEVER see a dead crow.

There is a reason for this. They are already dead.

CAT'S EYES

There is a small village in Sussex called Whispering Downs. It used to be a quiet backwater renowned for its rare birds and wild flowers. Then, a few years ago, some bright spark on Brighton Council decided to build a four-laned motorway on its doorstep, turning it from a beauty spot into a black spot. The graffiti daubed across the village sign said it all.

WHISPERING DOWNS
You have to be mad to live here!

Cat Clore lived there. She was a big girl. Ever since birth she'd been head and shoulders above other children of her age. This was good for some things like holding stolen sweets out of the reach of their owners, but it was also bad. Size turned Cat into a bully. She used her

bulk to get smaller children to do what she wanted. And there were no children smaller than her own brothers and sisters: Helen, Ian, Jacky, Barbara, Peter, Jocelyn and Tim. Tim was the last of the litter, born by accident and so teeny-tiny that aunts and uncles often remarked that Cat must have stolen the growing power out of his bones, because she was big and he was little. He was the height of a banister spindle.

When she started her gang Cat asked all of her brothers and sisters to be in it except for Tiny Tim.

'Who'd like to be in the Daredevils?' she asked, standing on an orange box in her father's garden shed. 'This is going to be the most exciting gang in the village. If you're not a member you'll be a nobody.'

'What's a nobody?' piped up Tiny Tim from the doorway.

'You!' snapped Cat. 'You're an embarrassing weed and there's only one thing to do with weeds – burn them!'

'Or put them down my pants if they're stinging nettles,' added Tiny Tim.

'Yes, that *was* rather a good torture, wasn't it?' chortled Cat. 'I don't want you within a million miles of my gang, Tim, because you'll turn us into a laughing stock.'

'Why are you suddenly starting a gang?' asked Helen.

'For fun and adventures!' lied Cat. The truth was she was starting a gang to be their leader, because leaders had to be obeyed. To persuade them to join up she gave each of her siblings a chocolate fairy cake and led them to believe that this was the sort of treat Daredevil members would be receiving on a regular basis. She didn't give a cake to Tiny Tim, however, and when he burst into tears the rest of his brothers and sisters felt sorry for him.

'If you want us to join you'll have to let Tim be a member too,' they said.

And because Cat was desperate to have seven slaves, she said, 'Oh all right then.' This was how Tiny Tim came to be a member of the Daredevils when he was the least brave boy in the village.

* * *

The gang met every Sunday in the shed. There were no cakes at the second meeting. The point of the gang wasn't that everyone ate cakes. That would have cost Cat money. The second meeting was all about Cat laying down the gang rules.

Rule 1. You cannot leave the gang unless you ride the big bull at North Farm in the nude.

This was a clever rule because it meant that she had this gang for life. Nobody ever rode the big bull because he killed dogs and everyone was thoroughly scared of it. Cat added the bit about being nude just in case someone was stupid enough to try.

Rule 2. All gang members must do everything the leader says.

When Helen put up her hand and said, 'But what if you tell us to do things we don't want to do?' Cat told her to not speak about this matter ever again, which was really clever, because Helen had to do everything her leader said.

Rule 3. To show the gang leader that you love her, you shall pay to her every week the sum of all of your pocket money.

It wasn't just Helen who protested at this rule. 'That's not fair!' they all shouted. Only Tiny Tim said nothing. Cat had been helping herself to his pocket money for years. Sensing a mutiny, Cat stood up and made a speech. 'If it could be any other way it would be,' she said. 'But if you don't like it, you know which way the bull is.' They did a bit more grumbling, but not much and none of it audible. They paid over their pocket money to be members of Cat's gang and were somehow made to feel grateful. In return for the money, she gave each of them a Gang Badge, a brown luggage label to tie onto their coats.

I AM A
DAIRDEVIL
FULLY PAID

Then she announced the final gang rule . . .

Rule 4. We're not called Daredevils for nothing. Every week we shall do daring things to prove to everyone in the village that Cat Clore must be the bravest girl in the village to be the leader of such a gang of daredevils.

'I need to work a bit more on the wording of this rule,' said Cat. 'But you get the gist.'

'What sort of daring things?' whispered Tiny Tim. His bottom lip was already trembling at the thought of doing anything dangerous.

'You know,' she said. 'Climbing trees, swinging on gates, running through the cemetery at night, damming the river with your wellies.'

'YOUR wellies?' queried Ian. 'You are going to be doing these daring things too, aren't you?'

'You haven't heard Rule 5 yet,' said Cat.

'I thought you said that Rule 4 was the final one,' grumbled Barbara.

'Actually, there are *two* more,' snapped Cat crossly.

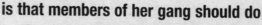

Rule 5. The leader can make up more final rules any time she likes.

Rule 6. (Which might be the final rule or it might not.) The leader does not have to do the daring things if she doesn't want to. The important thing is that members of her gang should do the daring things that make her look daring too and make her a hero in the eyes of all the children at school, so that they will want to be a member of her gang too and give her their pocket money too.

'Does the wording of that rule need a bit of working on too?' asked Jacky.

Cat took offence at this suggestion. 'Certainly not,' she huffed. 'That one's perfect.'

'It seems to me that you getting everyone's money is a bit of a theme to these rules,' said Peter.

'Rules is rules.' Cat smiled. 'They're not there to be liked.'

'So while we're doing all these dangerous things and giving you all our pocket money, what are you doing?' asked Jocelyn.

'Spending it,' said Cat.

'But that's not fair,' squeaked Tiny Tim. This was the second time he'd dared to speak without being spoken to first, so Cat slapped him. Being so big meant that she could slap anyone she liked and nobody ever slapped her back. This included the rest of her brothers and sisters, who were so scared of her slaps that when the meeting finished they gave her a jolly nice round of applause.

I've used this technique to control unruly blubbers and sicksters before. I call it the Slap-Them-Happy technique.

At the third meeting, Cat took everyone's money then taught the gang members the gang song . . .

Our leader is great
She is wise and adored
She's worth every penny
That we can afford.
We're happy to serve her
All the days long
Because in our eyes
She can do nothing wrong.

When it was pointed out that there was no mention of the Daredevils she added an extra verse, which she made up on the spot . . .

We're daring and devilish
Living life to the full
And if we don't like it
We can visit the bull.

'Happy now?' she said. 'Right. The task for this week is to do my homework.'

'I thought we were meant to do daring things,' said Peter.

'That's next week,' said Cat. 'Your leader has

spoken. Begone with you!'

* * *

But next week was darning Cat's socks; the week after that was sticking photographs into her photo album; and the week after that was giving her a beautifying makeover — washing her hair, polishing her nails and scrubbing the bits of hard skin off her toes with a pumice stone.

Don't trim me again!

Hemp Sock hates it when I trim his hair with a hedge-cutter

In fact, the pattern for every meeting thereafter was pretty much the same. Hand over the pocket money, sing the song and do chores for Cat. When the voices of protest became too loud she would take her Daredevils out to the gate in the field, tell them to stand on the top bar and throw themselves into the cow pats.

Nobody was allowed to say so, for fear of the leader's slap, but being a member of the Daredevils was a waste of time. What made matters worse were the lies that Cat told at school, in which she pretended that she was the bravest Daredevil of them all so that other children would join the club out of admiration for her and give her their pocket money. She would stand on a wooden crate next to the Science Labs and call everyone in to hear her porky tales of derring-do.

'Last Thursday I was rodeo-riding a llama, which is more dangerous than it sounds, because they can spit in your eye and give you an infection that turns your hair into wool or something. Then on Sunday I came face to face with a badger while I was doing a bit of illegal potholing. It tried to scratch my eyes out with its claws, but luckily I had read that the thing to do if you are stuck face down in a hole staring at an angry badger is to sing it *Two Little Boys* by Rolf Harris, because badgers love that song. So I did, and it worked. While it was singing along with the first chorus I punched its lights out!'

'Cor!' gurgled a boy called Snotty Shard. 'Is this what you do every week in the Daredevils?'

'If you don't believe me,' Cat said with a smile, 'ask my brothers and sisters. They'll tell you.' They had to.

If her brothers and sisters didn't smile and say, 'Oh yes, it's all true. Cat really is as brave as she says,' they got their teeth rearranged.

* * *

Then one day, a new boy appeared at the school. He was noticeable because he was Cat's size, which meant he wasn't scared of her. Cat was holding court as usual and telling everyone how she had been incredibly brave and slept overnight in the Big Cat cage at Brighton Zoo.

'If you don't go near them, they don't go near you,' she said blithely. 'There was only one moment that was a bit scary, when I woke up to find my head inside the jaws of a lion—'

'Rubbish!' said a voice in the crowd.

'Who said that?' roared Cat. 'Come here and say it to my face!'

So the new boy walked up to her and said, 'Rubbish! There isn't a Brighton Zoo.' This rather threw her. 'Are you saying that we don't do daring things in the Daredevils?' she said challengingly.

'I'm saying that there isn't a Brighton Zoo,' he said. 'And from that I am deducing "no". I don't think you do all the daring things you say you do.' Everyone was impressed with the way he used that word 'deducing' and the Daredevils loved watching Cat meet her match. 'I'll tell you what,' he went on.

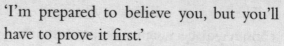

'I'm prepared to believe you, but you'll have to prove it first.'

And that was why, the following Sunday morning, the Daredevils found themselves standing on the grass verge by the side of the four-laned motorway. The new boy was there too to observe the daring feats and while the cars whizzed past like speeding bullets Cat kept telling him that he didn't need to stay.

'You've probably got Sunday lunch to get back for,' she said.

'No. Don't eat lunch. We have dinner at six,' he replied.

'All right, but your mum will probably be wondering where you are.'

He produced a mobile phone. 'She knows where I am,' he said. 'You're not trying to get rid of me so that you can sneak off home without doing anything daring, are you?'

'No!' protested Cat just a little bit too firmly so that everyone knew she really meant 'Yes!'

'So why are we here?' asked Tiny Tim. 'I'm cold.'

'Because,' shouted Cat as a lorry flashed past, 'today's dare is as follows. You have to run into the middle of the road, fill up your vest with gravel and run back.'

There was silence while the Daredevils considered the insanity of what their big sister was asking them to do.

'And who's stopping the traffic?' asked Peter.

The new boy laughed. 'Some daredevils you lot are!' he said.

'Nobody's stopping the traffic!' screamed Cat. 'It's a dare. We're the Daredevils!' Her gang members seemed a little unsure. 'OK,' said Cat. 'I'll make it easier for you. See those crows over there.'

Here we go!

She pointed to a dozen or so crows hopping on and off the motorway to fill their bellies with a hammered hedgehog. 'See how they never get hit. It's because of the way they move; always bouncing. Now look at these!' From her satchel she produced a pair of Wellington boots with springs glued to the bottom. 'I've made bouncing boots! So it's all perfectly safe.'

It was at this moment that the gang members started to shift awkwardly by the side of the road. Helen asked if she could go home and Ian said, 'Run those safety measures past us again.'

'Good heavens! Do I have to do all the thinking around here?' sneered Cat. 'Crows don't get hit because they can feel the cars coming by the tremors in their feet. These bouncing boots work in the same way. When a car gets close, they tremble.'

'I don't care what *they* do,' said Peter. 'I'm not doing it. You can slap me till the end of time, Cat, I'm not bouncing out in front of those cars to pick up gravel. You're off your rocker!'

Cat dragged Peter towards her and shoved her mouth into his ear. 'Look at him!' she whispered, pointing at the new boy. 'He's laughing at us. He doesn't think the Daredevils do daring things.'

'Well, we don't,' said Jacky. 'We do your chores mainly and jump off a gate.'

'I think I've proved my case,' smiled the new boy.

'No, you haven't!' shouted Cat. 'Helen, Ian, Barbara, Jocelyn . . . *you* do it!' They looked at each other nervously then shook their heads.

'Mum wouldn't like it,' said Barbara.

'Why don't you do it?' suggested Tiny Tim.

'Shut up!' yelled his big sister, slapping his ear with a loud thwack. 'You should all know this anyway, but I am forbidden to do it by Rule Number 7.' Helen pointed out that they only had *six* rules. 'And now we've got seven!' spat their glorious leader through gloriously gritted teeth.

Rule 7. The Law of Domino Potissimus (which loosely translates as, 'Your Glorious Leader Knows Best') does not allow the leader to do anything that might deprive her needy subjects of her wisdom and leadership.

'Are you sure that shouldn't be the Law of Scaredio Catissimus?' laughed the new boy. 'Which loosely translates as the Law of the Scaredy Cat!'

Taking courage from his outspokenness, the other members of the gang revolted.

'We're out too!' they said. 'You can't slap all of us. And we don't care if you call us cowards, because it's miserable being a member of your gang and we're better off out of it!'

The new boy looked puzzled. 'You're not cowards,' he said. 'Standing up to bullies is brave.'

In the space of ten seconds, Cat's authority had vanished. 'You're not walking out on me!' she frothed. 'You *will* cross that road and fill your vests with gravel!'

'It's over,' said Barbara. 'We've had enough of you. We're going home.'

'But you can't do this to me!' Cat howled. 'Somebody's got to walk through the traffic or the Daredevils will be finished and I'll be a laughing stock—Where are *you* going?!'

Tiny Tim was trying to walk off with the others when she grabbed him by the scruff of his neck. 'No!' he whimpered. 'I don't want to, Cat. I'm frightened.'

'Oi, you!' she shouted at the new boy. 'Stop right there! I'll show you how daring my gang is. This one's going to pick up the gravel right now!'

* * *

As Cat plonked her little brother's feet into the bouncing boots and swung him round to face the traffic, the crows lifted their beaks out of the hammered hedgehog and hopped briskly down the hard shoulder. They stopped in front of Cat and issued a warning with their cold, black-button eyes. Their stares said, 'Don't! Do not mess with cars.' The Daredevils heard them, the new boy heard them, but Cat only had ears for her own voice.

'Do as I say!' she bellowed, pushing her tiny brother into the road. As she did so, the crows flew up and pecked at her face. She flung up her arms to protect her eyes, letting go of Tiny Tim's shoulders. He stumbled backwards and fell off the bouncing boots while she crouched and ducked the jabbing beaks.

'Help me!' she cried, but it all happened so fast that nobody could move. Her eyes were closed. The bouncing boots were lying at her feet. As she tried to stand and run from the beaks, she tripped and fell forward into the path of an oncoming juggernaut.

* * *

In a bizarre twist of fate, the juggernaut that hit Cat was carrying lucky charms for Madame Rose, the fortune teller on Brighton Pier.

Actually she's a fortune MAKER, because if you cross her palm with silver she steals it!

You can decide for yourself if Cat's fate was lucky or not, but the fact remains that when the Police arrived at the scene of the accident they could not find Cat's body. They looked everywhere: in the bushes at the side of the road, under the lorry, even up on the power cables in case the impact had tossed her into the sky, but she was nowhere to be found. Because of this, nobody knew whether she had lived or died.

I'll give you a clue — she hadn't lived!

Had they looked more closely, they might have noticed that there was one more crow in that gang by the side of that four-laned motorway. And those that know, know that crows are the souls of children who play in the traffic.

Cat had been hit so hard by the lorry that her body had been driven deep into the tarmac like a fence post, until all that was visible above the road surface was the crown of her head and her sparkling eyes. Next time you drive down to Brighton, drive at night, and see if your headlights aren't reflected in Cat's eyes.

Part of Cat's down here now in the Hothell Darkness — her feet. That lorry must have hit her hard. because her head's still poking out the road and her feet are sticking through my ballroom ceiling, which means that her body must have stretched to over half a mile long. I must say, though, having her feet poking out is very useful at Christmas. Last year, I hung some mistletoe off her big TOE as a sort of a festive joke, but it backfired badly when the spoilt little brats refused to kiss under a pair of stinking, rotten feet. So I invented a compulsory game called 'Kiss or Lose Your Lips to this Cheese Grater!' and surprisingly all their objections vanished. I couldn't STOP them kissing until one of Cat's toes dropped off and the mistletoe fell into a girl's hair. We hung it back up on what was left of the foot and tried to rekindle the Christmas Spirit by calling it a different name, but kissing under the missing-toe wasn't the same at all.

Don't trim me again!

That's not the toe talking, that's Hemp-Sock again. Now if ever there was a blubber who deserved what he got, it was Hemp Sock; too posh for his own good. Born with a silver spoon in his mouth and died with a garden fork in his head. Actually, that's not true, because he's not entirely dead. Bits of him are still very much alive and covered in equal doses of shame and manure!

It was only a joke!

Please Look in the Mirror!

Slow down!

Don't trim me again!

Liquidate the plumber!

No Good Ever Comes of Wart!

THE HAIR FAIRIES

There was a Manor House just outside Totnes in Devon called Little Babylon. It was owned by the Duke of Devonshire, who was known as the Hippy Lord, because of the long hair which flowed down his back like a lion's mane. Little Babylon had the most splendid garden in all of England. The public flocked in their thousands to see the sculpted boxwood hedges which sprang from the earth in wild and wonderful shapes – snakes, sprites, dragons, trolls and dancing Grim Reapers. The Hippy Lord was much-praised for his Hedge-Art and unashamedly took all the credit.

'Oh yes,' he said when anybody bothered to ask. 'I've got a PhD in topiary. Took lessons from the Prince of Hedge-cutting himself, an Irish tinker known as Paddy the Shears.'

But the Hippy Lord was not as honest as he seemed. He was not the creator of these hedge sculptures. He said that he was, but knew that he wasn't.

* * *

The first child of the Hippy Lord was a son by his fifth wife, Sunrise. The boy's name was Hemp Sock: a hippy name born of his parents drinking too much dandelion wine at three in the morning. Because of his dazzling golden hair, which rippled like a field of corn, he was a spoilt child, who thought about little else but his own beauty.

'Is there anyone in the world quite as beautiful as me?' he said one day in the bath, while his mother massaged conditioning cream into the tips of his hair.

'Nobody,' beamed Sunrise. 'You are more beautiful than the stars in the heavens and the flowers in the Garden of Eden.'

'That's what I thought,' said Hemp Sock. So long as pictures of him were being published regularly in the Society magazine *Hair-lo!* he was the happiest little boy on the planet.

Talking of the Garden of Eden . . . Adam and Eve were sort of like the very first blubber and sickster on the planet. and they didn't get on either. LET THIS BE A WARNING TO YOU: If your sickster likes apples. leave home immediately! You could always come and live down here in The Darkness with me.

* * *

One day, whilst filming his son's hair for the family archives, the Hippy Lord asked him if he had ever wondered why he had such lovely hair.

'Because I do,' he said brusquely. 'It's the same as one cheetah running faster than all the others or one peacock having a lovelier fantail than the rest.

It's the law of the jungle. Somebody's got to be more perfect than everyone else and as far as little boys go that person just happens to be me.'

'That's not quite true,' said his father. 'You were given your hair by the Hair Fairies.'

'By the whom?' he said.

His hair may have been perfect but his grammar was not.

'The Hair Fairies,' chuckled his father carelessly. 'They were returning a favour.'

'Fairies!' gasped the boy. '*Real* fairies! With wings and stuff?'

'To be honest, I don't know,' said his father. 'I've never seen them. I've exchanged notes in coloured leaf dew, obviously, but they don't like to be seen.'

'Oh, but they wouldn't mind *me* seeing them,' he said. 'After all, they must like me to have given me such beautiful hair.'

'No,' said his father. 'You *never* want to see them.'

Used to getting his own way, Hemp Sock kicked up a strop. 'If you don't let me see them I shall scream,' he screamed.

'Scream away,' smiled his father. 'You can only see a Hair Fairy if you've been bad, and if you've been bad they have to punish you. Trust me, little prince, you *never* want to see a Hair Fairy.'

But Hemp Sock was curious. 'How bad would I

have to be to make a Hair Fairy appear?'

'This is silly,' said his father, who wished he'd never brought the subject up. 'Under no circumstances do you want a Hairy Fairy to appear, so you do not need to know.'

Hemp Sock was pretty sure he would have to do something awful to his hair; after all, it had been their gift to him. 'Why?' he said suddenly. 'Why did they give me my hair? If it was a gift, what was it a gift *for*?' His father shrugged as if he didn't know. He did. He knew everything, but he pretended that he didn't.

* * *

It sounds crazy that Hair Fairies, flighty creatures of diminished stature, weighing in at six and a half nanograms with a reach no longer than a chewed match stick, the wing span of an aphid and the body mass of a banana prawn, could threaten the life of a human being. But size isn't everything, and if you've got mischief, magic, the ability to plug power tools into your limbs, extensive topiary skills and a natural gift for dancing on your side, that's pretty much all you need to be a master race.

The very next day Sunrise announced that she was pregnant, and nine months later Hemp Sock had a sister. Like her brother, Moonunit was born with a shock of hair on top of her head. Unlike her brother the hair was inky black and by the time she was one it flowed down her back like precious oil. Wig-makers rushed from around the world to outbid each other for a snip of her crowning glory. But it was not for sale.

'It's a gift from the Hair Fairies,' Hemp Sock announced to the greedy collectors. 'Nobody must ever cut off my sister's hair!'

'Good boy,' beamed his father the Hippy Lord, thinking that his son had learned his lesson well. But Hemp Sock was a good actor. He gave the outward appearance of being protective of his younger sister, but underneath, he was a seething ball of bile and fury waiting to explode. So jealous was he of his snotty sister stealing his limelight that every day he plotted his revenge in devilishly dark corners.

There are plenty of those down here!

* * *

For three long years he fooled the world into

74

thinking that he adored his sister. When people told him how privileged he was to live in the same house as her hair he nodded and laughed gaily. When shifty strangers slipped him cash to snip them a curl he pushed the money back into their hands. When children pulled her hair at school he broke their fingers. Hemp Sock was the perfect elder brother; loyal, loving and generous to a fault.

But that was all about to change. When Moonunit turned four, she became old enough to know better, and *old enough to know better* was exactly what Hemp Sock had been waiting for.

* * *

It was a cold Monday in late March. The Hippy Lord was out in the garden attending to the latest hedge sculpture to have popped up overnight – a phoenix rising from the ashes – and Sunrise was *Greeting the Sun* in a variety of yoga positions on the hearth rug. This meant that Hemp Sock could do as he pleased without anyone knowing his business. He found Moonunit brushing her hair in the nursery underneath a hair humidifier.

'Do you like secrets?' he said, kneeling in front of her and stroking her cheek.

'I don't like secrets,' beamed his sister. 'I *love* them!'

He pulled her onto his lap and whispered into her ear. 'Your hair was a gift to you from the Hair Fairies.'

'I know that,' she said. So far so true.

'And these fairies are fun loving creatures; real practical jokers.'

'Really?' she said as the truth started to bend.

'Oh yes,' he declared authoritatively. 'It upsets them when they *never* see you having fun with their gift.'

'You mean they don't want me to brush my hair?'

'Or wash it, or cream it or do anything boring to make it look nicer.' His tongue flicked in and out of his mouth like a wily serpent's. 'Would you like to do some hairdressing . . . with a difference?'

'If it will please the Hair Fairies,' she said.

'Oh it *will*,' he reassured her, adding darkly, 'but only if you promise to say that *you* did it.'

Moonunit wasn't sure she'd understood. 'Say that I did what?'

'Whatever it is that we do to your hair to have fun!' squealed Hemp Sock. 'Look, I can help you, but you can't tell anyone that I did.'

'And if I *do*?'

'Then the Hair Fairies will kill you.'

'*Kill* me?'

'Stone dead with a bullet.'

Moonunit's bottom lip wobbled. 'Chin up!' cried her big brother. 'It hasn't happened yet.'

'And if I *don't* tell anyone that you had a hand in it?' she asked, bravely.

'Then the Hair Fairies will laugh at your joke,' said Hemp Sock, 'and will give you even more beautiful hair to reward you for the fun you've brought into their lives.' Moonunit scratched her nose.

'Hair Fairies are complicated creatures,' she said.

'Not when you know them as well as I do,' lied Hemp Sock. 'Shall we have some fun and play hairdressers?'

Not realising the danger, Moonunit slipped her hand into her big brother's and trustingly followed him into the garden.

* * *

He laid her on the lawn and rinsed her hair in some smelly green water from a watering can, before rubbing in copious amounts of mud and snails.

'Having fun?' he enquired.

'Sort of,' she said doubtfully. They he sat her up so

that he could give her his 'special plaits'. Only they weren't plaits, they were knots: big, wet knots, pulled tight to cause his little sister maximum pain.

'Ow!' she yelled. 'That's hurting!'

'Fun always does,' he smirked. 'Don't move. I know just the thing to take the pain away.' He ran into the kitchen, took a plate out of the fridge and returned to the garden. 'Cold mashed potato and beans,' he said, upturning the plate onto her head and rubbing last night's supper into her hair until all of the tomato sauce had been absorbed. 'How's that?'

'Cold,' she whimpered.

'Then what you need is some piping hot custard,' he squeaked gleefully, jumping to his feet and rushing back indoors to use the microwave.

* * *

Half an hour later, Moonunit was unrecognisable. It looked like a giant ogre with an unstoppable tummy bug had thrown up over her head.

'Who's got the most beautiful hair *now*?' snickered Hemp Sock under his breath, as his mother danced into the garden trailing a pink veil.

'Who did this?' she wailed when she saw

her daughter's head. Hemp Sock shot his sister a piercing stare and mouthed the words 'Hair Fairies'.

'I did,' she said proudly, and because she was now four and *old enough to know better,* her mother believed her. In a fury, she turned the hose on her trifle-headed daughter, then banished her to her bedroom. Moonunit left the garden howling.

'I tried to stop her, but she wouldn't listen,' said Hemp Sock innocently.

'I thought you probably had,' said his mother. 'You're a good boy.'

'I am, aren't I?' said Hemp Sock. 'So do you love me?'

'Of course I do,' his mother said distractedly as she headed back indoors.

'More than Moonunit?' called the boy. But his mother was already weeping in the kitchen and did not reply.

Hemp Sock was not satisfied with this reaction. He had expected Moonunit to be thrown out of the house and sent to live in the pig sty, or even better with foster parents. Clearly messing up the hair was not enough. If Moonunit was to fully fall from grace, leaving Hemp

Sock as the favoured child once again, he would need to go further. *Much* further! If Moonunit's hair was so beautiful, then Moonunit's hair had to go!

Liquidate the plumber!

You'll have to forgive Kitty and Winnie. Ever since they were pulped pink they've been going ever-so-slightly round the U-bend.

Ten minutes later, when Hemp Sock crept into his sister's bedroom, he had a pair of scissors in hand.

'How are you doing?' he asked sympathetically. His sister was lying in a puddle of snot and tears on the bed.

'Not good,' she sobbed.

'You'll feel much better when I tell you this,' he said, sitting down next to her like her only true friend in the world. 'The Hair Fairies appeared in the garden just after you'd left and told me what a hoot they thought the messing up of the hair was.' Moonunit's face brightened. 'But—' he went on '—although they thought it was a good first effort, they didn't think you'd gone far enough.'

'How much further can I go?' pined his sister.

He produced the scissors from behind his back. 'Snip snip,' he said. 'All off!'

'All off!'

'I knew you'd be grateful,' said Hemp Sock. 'Now remember, for the Hair Fairies to gift you even more beautiful hair as a reward for giving them a laugh, you have to say it was you what did it.'

There was that grammar again. I don't know; all that posh edukashon for nuffink!

'But what about mummy and daddy?' asked the girl. 'Won't they be cross?'

'Not when they see your *new* hair, even more lustrous and beautiful than before. They'll thank you!'

Moonunit wasn't sure at all, so her big brother made up her mind for her. He grabbed a handful of her hair, tugged her roughly towards him and, ignoring her shrieks, snipped off the first clump. 'There's no going back now!' he yelled as the blades swooped and flashed and exposed the pinkness of her scalp.

* * *

Hearing their daughter's cries, the Hippy Lord and his fifth wife burst into the bedroom. The first thing they saw was their daughter's hair on the floor and the scissors in her hand.

'What have you done?' roared the Hippy Lord.

'Cut off my hair,' she sobbed. Despite the fact that lying did not come easily to her, Moonunit remained loyal to her brother. More than could be said for him.

'Oh Moonunit!' he cried. 'What a naughty daughter she is, don't you think, daddy?'

But the Hippy Lord was not convinced by what he'd seen. 'If you were cutting off your own hair, why were you crying out for help?' he asked.

Moonunit had not anticipated this question and could not think of a reply.

'She wasn't crying out for *help*,' jumped in Hemp Sock. 'She was crying out for *hell*! Send me to hell for what I am doing to my hair!' he cried, mimicking Moonunit's voice. 'Oh, bad Moonunit! Leave the house and never come back! Begone, you naughty hair chopper. I'm the only child our parents love now!'

In the face of such bare-faced

betrayal even Moonunit had to break her promise. 'But you told me to,' she howled, drawing a startled look of panic from her brother.

'You don't mean that,' he said quickly.

'Yes I do,' bellowed his bald sister. 'You made me. You did it when I wasn't ready.'

'*Me!*' he exclaimed. 'You lying wretch! She's trying to blame me, daddy. I wasn't even here.'

The Hippy Lord grabbed his son's hands and turned them over. 'So what is this black hair doing under your fingernails?'

Hemp Sock tried to bluff it out. 'I've been stroking a horse's tail,' he said boldly.

'Since when did we keep horses?' asked his mother.

'It's a lie,' seethed the Hippy Lord. 'Because he's jealous of his sister's hair!'

'No!' he cried. But he *was* and the silence that followed condemned him.

'Did I not tell you,' hissed his father, 'that if you sullied the Hair Fairies' gift they would take their revenge?'

'Yes, you did,' replied Hemp Sock recklessly. 'Like I'm *really* scared of a fairy!'

'You should be,' said his mother.

'Why?' sneered Hemp Sock. 'Whoops, sorry little fairy, I've just trodden on your head!'

'You have ruined Little Babylon!' his mother shouted back. 'You have insulted the fairies and now they will leave.'

'Oh fairies, fairies, fairies!' yelled Hemp Sock. 'Why can't we just forget about the fairies and talk about *me*?'

'But the fairies *are* you,' his mother replied. 'Everything you see around you, everything we have is only here *because* of the Hair Fairies.'

'Now you're talking nonsense,' laughed Hemp Sock. 'Could you please just answer the question – do you or don't you love me more than Moonunit?'

His parents did not reply.

'I've got lovely hair, she's got none. You *must* like me more!'

'No,' said his father. 'Right now I think we like you less.'

*　*　*

That did it. After everything he'd done to make his parents love him . . .

'Like me *less*!' he screamed as he stumbled into the garden and tore open the door to the shed where his father kept his tools. 'I'll give you a *real*

84

reason to like me less!' He emerged with a pair of garden shears and with one vicious slice cut through the trunk of the nearest boxwood bush. As the Grim Reaper toppled forward onto his green and leafy face, Hemp Sock flitted through the garden like an avenging moon-shadow, and made his parents pay for their betrayal with the blades of his shears.

One hour later, as the sun set on an orgy of destruction, the Hippy Lord's work lay in ruins on the ground: boxwood sculptures smashed and splintered, disfigured and destroyed. No more phoenix, no more dragons, no more trolls. The sculpted boxwood hedges which had sprung from the earth in wild and wonderful shapes and for which Little Babylon had become famed were gone, and Hemp Sock had exacted his terrible revenge.

But as he stood in the middle of the lawn catching his breath, he heard the plaintive sound of a flute interlaced with the sorrowful cry of a violin. It was coming from the meadow known as the Fairy Ring. As he peered into the darkness he saw a dim light and a troop of tiny marching figures. At first he thought they were stag beetles, but then he saw their translucent wings and porcelain faces with miniature eyes and ears. They were fairies. Thousands of them in black caps, marching in step like soldiers at a State Funeral. At the heart of the parade was a group of fairies draped in a spider's web. On their shoulders was a lily pad and on the lily pad was a wooden coffin. They walked solemnly towards a hole in the ground into which they lowered the coffin. Suddenly a black puffball of fairies appeared in the sky with a boxwood hedge suspended on vines below it. The hedge was dropped into the hole above the coffin, its roots were covered in soil and the procession fanned out around the grave. Sixty larger fairies with muscular arms and four wings now stepped forward. Bolted to each of their wrists was a metre-long, serrated blade. Raising these weapons above their heads, the warrior fairies – for that is what they looked like to Hemp Sock – flew to the top of the bush, where, in a whirlwind of flying leaf and twig, they worked their way down towards the ground, re-shaping the hedge into a perfect likeness of Hemp Sock. He recognised himself immediately and gasped. This was *his* funeral.

* * *

As one, the fairies turned to face him. Their hate-filled eyes sent a shiver of fear down the boy's spine. He sensed danger and tried to run, but his feet had rooted to the ground. A fairy wearing a golden cape flew forward from the circle.

'If you can see us,' it said, 'you have been bad. If you have been bad you must be punished.' Hemp Sock's voice had all but disappeared.

'Me?' he squeaked.

'Was it you who spurned our gift?'

'No,' he cried. 'I never touched *my* hair. I've always loved my hair. I'm grateful that you gave it to me.'

'But you cut off your sister's?'

'An accident,' whimpered Hemp Sock. With their hedge-trimmer hands glinting, the warrior-fairies flew forward and hovered in front of the boy's face. 'Please don't cut me,' he squealed.

'For fifty years we have lived in harmony with Little Babylon,' boomed the golden fairy. 'Your father allowed us to use this garden as our burial ground.'

With horror, Hemp Sock suddenly realised what

he had done. His father was not a topiarist. That was his secret. He had never shaped a hedge in his life. It was the fairies who created the hedge sculptures, shaping boxwood headstones for their dead. In return they had given the Hippy Lord and his children the most beautiful hair in the world. 'But *you* do not like our gift. You think it is yours to destroy on a whim.'

'Not at all,' protested Hemp Sock. 'I'm sorry.'

The muscular fairies with the hedge chopping arms switched on their blades.

'Too late,' said the golden fairy. 'You have dishonoured our dead. We must now leave this place and seek another, while you must remain as a warning to all who might follow your path.' Pushing its cape behind its arms the golden fairy nodded its head. The warriors flew in a hypnotic configuration in front of Hemp Sock's eyes, while the foot soldiers danced around his legs, wailing like parents at a child's funeral. Although they were only small their voices were large. The rhythmic pounding of their feet grew louder in Hemp Sock's ears while the blades of the warriors flashed before his eyes and their wings buzzed like a death squad of wasps. Hemp Sock tried to scream, but his lips would not move; nor his arms nor his legs.

* * *

When his parents found him in the morning he had turned to petrified wood. There was an inscription carved into his chest.

> Here he lies
> The boy who thought
> Our gift of hair
> Was worth but nought.

Little Babylon closed down three weeks later. Once the Hair Fairies had moved on in search of another burial ground the gardens fell to wrack and ruin. With no more boxwood sculptures to see the public stopped coming. The Hippy Lord, his fifth wife Sunrise and their daughter Moonunit, whose hair grew back in time for the Summer Solstice, moved to Monmouthshire, where they bought a Garden Centre which specialised in badly - sculpted Bonsai trees and went out of business within a year.

As for Hemp Sock, he now lives down here in the Hothell Darkness garden. I call it a garden, but it's more of an overgrown cemetery. It's where all the Children of the Night sleep, the ones who can't eat solids and don't like daylight. I kidnapped Hemp Sock from the meadow formerly known as the Fairy Ring, where the Hair Fairies had left him. He was a solitary unmoving figure carved from a boxwood hedge and had long green hair and two leafy tears rolling silently down his knotted face!

A mysterious thing happened when I got him down here, though. His hair fell out! How AMUSING is that! It was because I paid a fox to pee on his trunk. Day after day it emptied its bladder over his roots, until eventually all that acid got into Hemp Sock's veins and turned his leaves brown. And a week after that they fell off. So now he's bald, which I think serves him right, because Moonunit was a good sickster.

THE WATERMELON BABIES

Once upon a time, in a country not so very different from this one, there was a terrible drought. Politicians had ignored the scientists' warnings about global warming, and now those warnings had come true; rivers had run dry, crops had failed and any child who did not wear sun cream shrivelled to the size of a raisin. In fact it stayed so hot for so long that vultures flew in from afar like eager tourists and found the larder well stocked with man meat.

The government passed laws to preserve the dwindling water supply, but it was too little too late. **SAVE WATER** their posters said:

NO SWIMMING POOLS
NO WATER FEATURES
NO HOSE PIPES

As the crisis deepened their advice grew more desperate.

SAVE WATER
DRINK YOUR OWN WEE-WEE

* * *

In an otherwise ordinary town called Waterbrook, one garden stood out from all the rest. Instead of dead plants and brown lawns, the flowers bloomed, the grass was green and frogs frolicked in the puddles of water underneath the rhubarb leaves. This garden belonged to two thoughtless step-sisters, called Kitty and Winnie Camel. Before their parents had married, the two girls had been brought up alone, without brothers or sisters. The most important thing in each girl's life had been herself. Now that they were step-sisters they found it hard sharing the attention and as a result life was one long competition to prove who was the best. Who was the fastest? Who was the cleverest? Who could fire the longest stream of water from their SuperSoaker?

'Aaaagh! You're wetting my hair!' shrieked Kitty, as their water fight spilled out of the kitchen into the garden. 'Winnie! No!'

Winnie had dropped her gun and picked up a bucket of water. 'Take that!' she shrieked, wasting two good gallons over her no-good step-sister's head.

'Right!' gasped Kitty. 'You've asked for this!' And without a thought for the ban she turned on the garden tap and soaked Winnie with the hosepipe. They weren't stupid. They knew that water was precious, but thought that saving it was what *other people* did.

Despite Mrs Camel's best efforts to curtail Kitty and Winnie's water wastage, the step-sisters refused point blank to change their daily routines.

'If she can do it, so can I!' was a cry heard several times a day from the bathroom. Because Kitty always washed her clothes every night so did Winnie, and because Winnie was used to taking three baths a day and washing her hair every morning Kitty insisted on doing the same.

'We don't want to stink,' Winnie said.

'Girls are fragrant,' said Kitty. 'Not like boys who smell of cheese.'

And they kept the tap running while they brushed their teeth. Their mother told them countless times to half fill a tooth mug with water and rinse their mouths out with that, but they wouldn't listen. So she tied one end of a piece of string around the tap and kept the other end in her pocket. This meant that wherever she was in the house, it only took a surreptitious tug on the string and she could turn the tap off!

* * *

One Tuesday morning, Winnie's mouth was still foaming with toothpaste when the Phantom-Tap-Tugger struck.

'It doesn't matter if I leave the water running!' she screamed down the stairs, cutting the string with a pair of nail scissors and switching the tap back on again. 'It's only a little dribble.'

'If everyone left their taps running we'd soon have no water at all,' her mother shouted from the kitchen.

'But they don't!' shrieked Winnie.

'That's not the point! All the little dribbles would add up to one big stream. Eventually, whole rivers would go to waste.'

'I wish you'd dribble away!' Winnie yelled, making herself hot under the collar. So hot, in fact, that she ran downstairs to retrieve a can of chilled spring water from the fridge and sprayed a cooling mist all over her face. 'Aaaah!' she sighed. 'That's better!'

Mrs Camel had never seen anything quite so surplus to requirements in all her life. Of all the unnecessary things that her self-centred daughter owned 'Indoor Rain' took the biscuit. 'Where did you get that from?' she gasped.

'*I* bought it,' said Mr Camel sheepishly as he crept in through the back door. 'Winnie said she couldn't live without it.' When Mr Camel had gained an extra daughter he had lost his sense of reason.

* * *

It would be fair to say (as Mrs Camel did rather often) that Mr Camel spoiled his girls rotten. At the start of the most recent summer term, for example, Kitty had a notion to be a diving champion. So Mr Camel built her a Water Park in the garden. No matter that the rest of the country had no water to drink; he built his beloved daughter an Olympic-sized swimming pool containing 13.5 metric tonnes of water, two fixed diving boards, a spring board, one vertical slide called The Leap of Death, and a lazy river. But of course neither girl was happy if the other was getting all of the attention. So Winnie decided that she wanted to water-ski. What did he do? He knocked down the slides and bought a speedboat, which he launched across the pool with Winnie in tow.

'That's not fair,' sulked Kitty, as Winnie was dragged around the pool for the five hundred and sixteenth time. 'You're only her step-daddy, but you're behaving like you're her *real* daddy. I want to be a famous ice dancer!' Out with the speedboat, in with the freezer gun. Kitty's father froze the water in the pool, bought Kitty a fur-lined skating dress and some buckskin blades and told Winnie to stand aside.

'Sorry, Winnie,' jeered Kitty as she practised her triple lutz. 'I haven't stopped you waterskiing, have I?' But pride always comes before a fall, especially in ice skating, and after one fall too many Kitty refused to get up.

'Are you all right, Princess?' asked Mr Camel.

'I'm cold!' chattered Kitty . . .

As if ice skating was ever going to be hot!

. . . and Winnie saw her chance.

'I *love* cold,' she shouted. 'I want a ski slope!' So Mr Camel dammed up the nearest river and diverted the precious water into a snow machine, which sprayed the garden with artificial snowflakes that stuck together to form a slope. As Mrs Camel watched through the kitchen window, she was horrified. For as long as Winnie and Kitty hogged all the water, someone elsewhere was going without.

* * *

Then, one Friday morning, the water dried up completely. The taps clanked and shuddered as the pipes filled with air. Kitty and Winnie were infuriated by the sheer inconvenience of having no water and refused to go to school.

'My clothes are filthy!' shouted Kitty.

'And my hair is so dirty,' moaned Winnie, 'that I look like a bird's nest!' Then the two step-sisters locked themselves in their bedroom and announced to their parents that they wouldn't be coming out until they could hear the sound of running water again.

If it was just the sound of running water they wanted I could always have lent them my fox!

A few minutes later, after a flick through the *Yellow Pages* to find a plumber, a man stepped out of a green van outside the house. He worked for the Watermelon Plumbing Company.

'Lady.' The plumber tipped his cap to Mrs Camel when she opened the door.

'You were quick,' she said.

'I was waiting outside when I got your call,' he explained.

'Waiting outside! Why?'

'Heard you had a problem with thoughtless daughters. Thought I could . . . erm . . .' The plumber checked nervously over his shoulder. 'Help.' Then he took out a harmonica, played a single note to pitch himself and sang . . .

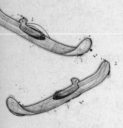

> *If it's water from a stone*
> *Or a lesson what you seek*
> *Trust the Watermelon Plumber*
> *For to make the pip-lets squeak!*

Mrs Camel had never met a singing plumber before. 'Pip-lets?' she asked.

'Pips off the old block,' he said. Mrs Camel was none the wiser, but he did seem to be offering her daughters a lesson of some sort, and *that* caught her interest.

* * *

After lying under the sink for ten minutes and making various tut-tut noises to emphasise the complexity of the problem, the Watermelon Plumber removed his head from inside the cupboard.

'Tell you what the problem is, lady. You didn't oughtas let your daughters use up all your waters! Ha ha!'

'That's what I've been saying!' said Mrs Camel, fixing her husband with a look of cold recrimination. 'I told you we'd run out of water if we didn't ration it.' The plumber had disappeared back inside the cupboard.

'Mark my words, as sure as sewage flows into the sea,' he said, 'if those girls don't mend their ways and start thinking about other folk, they'll come to a sticky end.'

'What do you mean, sticky end?' asked Mrs Camel, but the plumber ignored her and chortled instead.

'Hello!' he said. 'There may not be water in these pipes, but there's *something* up here.'

'A blockage?' asked Mr Camel, hopefully. The

plumber slid out from under the sink again, only this time with a black seed in each hand.

'No,' he said. 'Watermelon seeds.'

'Watermelon seeds!?' exclaimed his audience.

'And me a Watermelon Plumber. What are the chances of that happening?' he chuckled unconvincingly. 'Still, I can think of worse things to grow in a drought.'

He was not wrong. If water pipes could no longer deliver water to the family, the next best thing was surely watermelons.

'Why?' sulked Kitty.

'Because if you don't drink water,' said the plumber, 'you'll end up dying like a dried-out dingo in a sandstorm. If, on the other hand, you grow these two seeds into watermelons then you can grow more watermelons from *their* seeds and you'll have a never-ending supply of water.'

'All very nice,' sneered Winnie, 'but I can't wash my hair in a watermelon, can I?'

'It's not always about you,' said the plumber.

'And I can't wash my clothes,' said Kitty. 'I know what your game is. You're a lousy plumber and don't know how to get our water back, so you're telling us this stupid watermelon story to make sure we don't phone your boss and get you sacked!'

'I *am* my boss,' he said. 'And if you don't do what I say, *you'll* be the ones who come to a sticky end.'

'You said that before,' said Mrs Camel.

'Then it must be true,' said the plumber, picking up his tools. 'And here's what I say: grow the watermelons and give them to your friends to eat.'

'What about *us*?' screeched the girls. 'Don't we get a piece?'

'No,' smiled the plumber. 'You'll go thirsty, but at least you'll have a warm glow in your hearts from helping others.' Winnie and Kitty could not see the point of this and refused to co-operate, so the plumber put it another way. 'Why don't you girls have a competition?' he said. 'See which of you can grow the juiciest watermelon, then take them both into school for your friends to decide.' It was a masterstroke. The prospect of a *competition* had the step-sisters frothing with excitement, as well the plumber knew it would!

* * *

For two weeks the plumber's plan to reform the step-sisters went well. In the warmth of the airing cupboard the two watermelons grew fast, and on the Monday morning, Kitty and Winnie staggered into school with heavy rucksacks.

'Good morning, children,' said the weary teacher, 'and it *is* a good morning. I know how thirsty you all are, but today our good friends, Kitty and Winnie, have something they'd like to share with us.'

Kitty and Winnie took the watermelons out of their rucksacks, walked to the front of the class and placed them carefully on the teacher's desk. Sixty eyes followed the juice. Thirty tongues dribbled.

'Hello,' said Winnie. 'This is my watermelon in front of me.'

'And this is mine,' said Kitty.

A boy called Herman put up his hand. 'Is it true that we're each going to be given a piece to eat?' he asked.

'That's right,' smiled the teacher.

'Then can I have a piece of Winnie's watermelon, because it looks juicier than Kitty's?'

That was all it took; one careless comment to refuel the step-sisters' rivalry and the plumber's warning was forgotten!

'Yes, you're right!' crowed Winnie. 'Mine *is* juicier, isn't it?'

'No it's not!' howled Kitty. 'How dare you say that? Mine's the best!'

'Well, there's only one way to find out,' jeered her step-sister, pulling a carving knife out of her rucksack. Then she chopped her watermelon into ten thick slices and ate them all, declaring with each bite, 'Hmmm delicious! So juicy. I've never tasted anything so sweet and lovely in my life.' Not to be outdone, Kitty did the same with her watermelon and crammed the pink flesh into her mouth as fast as she could.

'So watery!' she cried. 'Mmmmmm. Look at the juice running down my chin. Your watermelon is like a dried up old sock compared to mine, Winnie!' In less than a minute, the selfish sisters had devoured the two watermelons. When they'd finished they looked up to see their thirsty classmates in tears.

'What are you lot crying at?' yelled Kitty. 'They weren't your watermelons anyway. They were ours!'

'That's right!' mocked Winnie. 'So stop blubbing!'

'Yeah!' laughed Kitty. 'You're all selfish cry-babies, because tears are a huge waste of water!'

* * *

Outside the school, in a parking bay reserved for Avenging Artisans, the Watermelon Plumber put a tick next to their names in a little pink book.

That's 'tick' as in mark of affirmation. not blood sucking parasite! If it had been a parasite it would have burst when he closed the covers and splattered his windscreen in blood.

That night, as the moon turned a shade of watermelon red, strange things occurred in Kitty and Winnie's bedroom. As the step-sisters slept, their bodies swelled like balloons until their arms and legs had completely disappeared and their skin had thickened and turned green. In the cold light of morning, the horrible truth was told. Kitty and Winnie had turned into watermelons!

Mr Camel was more upset than Mrs Camel, but he soon got over it when he realised that his precious daughters weren't actually dead. He carried the two watermelons downstairs and placed them on the window sill in the sitting room, where Mrs Camel watered their roots to keep them alive.

'Ah well,' said Mr Camel. 'Best be off to work.'

'Me too!' said Mrs Camel, brightly. 'Have a nice day, girls.'

'WAIT!' bellowed Kitty. 'Don't leave us here in the window for everyone to see!'

'Especially not when they're so thirsty!' shouted Winnie. But people can't hear watermelons when they speak and Mr and Mrs Camel were no exception.

This meant that when school broke up at three o'clock, and Kitty and Winnie's parched classmates walked home, Kitty and Winnie were sitting in the window for all of them to see. Except that when they stopped outside the Camel house, they didn't see Kitty and Winnie at all.

'Watermelons!' they gasped, with greedy eyes that stood out on stalks.

It took just one brick to smash the window, and thirty thirsty tongues, before Kitty and Winnie were watermelons no more. When they had drunk their fill, Kitty and Winnie's school friends skipped off home, leaving the pavement covered in chewed red slices of watermelon, which Mr and Mrs Camel trod in when they came home from work.

And if that's not a sticky end I don't know what is.

This next tale has a sticky end too. Actually, it's more gooey with a terminal stench of putrefaction. The sort of slow-drip effect you might get if you'd gone on a six-week summer cycling tour of Europe and forgotten you were carrying a severed foot in your rucksack. By the time you got home that foot would be running around inside your PVC lining like melted ice cream and would smell worse than a nineteenth-century goat's cheese. That's the sort of ending this next story's got.

No Good Ever Comes of Wart!

Oh. I don't know. It got rid of you two blubbers!

Before we move on to Tom and Jerry. I haven't finished telling you about Kitty and Winnie. I scraped up what I could find of them in the cracks between the paving slabs and rushed them down here where they belong. I racked my brains for weeks trying to think of nasty things to do to two teaspoons of mulched-up watermelon. but I was all out. And then I had it! Perfume! Air Freshener! So now I keep them in a can with essence of skunk and spray them about a bit when the smell of sulphur gets too much.

Now some blubbers are really close. I call them Blood Blubbers. But some blubbers hate each others guts. I call them Tom and Jerry.

THE NUCLEAR WART

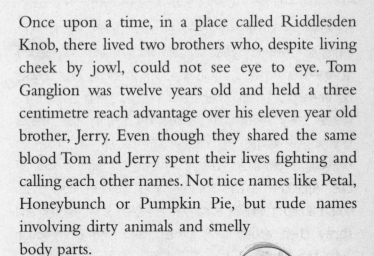

Once upon a time, in a place called Riddlesden Knob, there lived two brothers who, despite living cheek by jowl, could not see eye to eye. Tom Ganglion was twelve years old and held a three centimetre reach advantage over his eleven year old brother, Jerry. Even though they shared the same blood Tom and Jerry spent their lives fighting and calling each other names. Not nice names like Petal, Honeybunch or Pumpkin Pie, but rude names involving dirty animals and smelly body parts.

'Worm!'
'Weasel!'
'Toad!'
'Pig!'

'Pig's armpit!'

'Baboon's bum!'

'Fawning pie-dog!'

'Fawning pie-dog! What's that?'

'A fawning pie-dog, Mr Sponge-brain, is a chess-playing dog who eats pies!'

'Chess-playing!'

'Yes, chess-playing. King to Fawn three. Checkmate. Over and out!'

'I think you'll find, Mr Polystyrene-Loft-Insulation-Brain, that's Pawn not Fawn!'

'What did you just call me?'

'You heard, worm!'

'Weasel!'

'Toad!'

'Pig!' And so it went on, round and round in a never-ending vicious circle.

* * *

The brothers regularly came to blows, and although kicking and punching were their two favourite methods of making a point, they were also no strangers to slapping, dead-legging, nose-twisting, Chinese burns, Full Nelsons and even, on occasion, hair pulling. They broke precious vases, knocked paintings off walls, ripped curtains, kicked chunks out of sofas, and smashed plates and windows almost every day. But of course it was always the other one's fault.

As you might imagine, they were difficult to live with; doubly so, because Tom and Jerry's parents detested violence. Their father was a peace campaigner who designed placards for CND. **STOP THE WAR** and **BAN THE BOMB** were two of his. Their mother was a feng shui consultant who specialized in rearranging furniture to help people live in harmony with their environment. So Mrs Ganglion had moved the furniture in the boys' bedroom to help her sons get on. She had ripped out the hand basin, because water leads to illness and misfortune; she had placed a crystal globe in the Northeast corner of the room for good luck; and she had spent an entire weekend making sure that their wardrobe doors were the same size.

'The son with the bigger door will have an inclination towards mistreating the one with the smaller door,' she told her husband.

'Well, I never!' chuckled Mr Ganglion.

'No, you never did,' said his wife rather brittly. 'That's why I'm the feng shui expert and you're not.' It would be fair to say that because of the boys' fighting, the atmosphere in the house was like crab-apple jelly – never less than strained.

* * *

Tom and Jerry fought like cat and mouse. It never took more than a casual look or half a word to spark an assault. Fights erupted from the tiniest things: who had the largest scoop of mash; whose swimming trunks were less baggy; who left the comic in the loo; and perhaps the best of all, the day that Jerry punched Tom for looking like he *might* do something horrid.

'Stop it!' cried their mother as Tom grabbed Jerry's ear lobe and twisted.

'Say you're sorry.'

'I'm sorry!' screamed Jerry, but when a triumphant Tom let go he added, '. . . for saying sorry that I hurt you! Ha!' Then he flicked Tom's forehead with a wooden ruler and kicked him in the shin.

'Stop it!' yelled their mother for a second time. 'Don't you see what you're doing?'

'What?' cried the brothers, freezing in a tug-of-shirts.

'You're creating a huge negative energy field.'

'It was *his* fault,' said Tom.

'It doesn't matter whose fault it was!' she snapped. 'Thanks to you two this house is infected with bad karma. How many times do I have to tell you that badness builds up? It doesn't drift away like clouds. It lies around like mud waiting to slip you up!' Neither boy could have cared less. 'Where do you think it's going, all your hate and fury? I'll tell you where . . . skulking, lurking, lying in ambush, somewhere deep within these four walls.'

'Feng phoooey!' sneezed Tom with an exaggerated flick of his head.

'Bless you,' sniggered Jerry.

'Don't mock me,' seethed their mother. 'Somewhere, too close for comfort, is a hoard of fermenting evil!' But her sons had grown bored of her same-old lectures and were fighting again; this time over a packet of Love Hearts.

'Where are they, thief?' Tom was trying to squeeze the information out of his younger brother's skull by crushing his neck in a headlock. Mrs Ganglion sighed and left the room. She tried her best to keep them apart, but her best was never good enough, which was a shame, because the following day she was proved right!

* * *

The situation flared up at lunchtime when Jerry wanted to make the French dressing for the salad.

Tom was incensed. 'You make rubbish dressing!' he shouted. 'It tastes of cat's pee!'

'I like it.'

'You like the Eurovision Song Contest. That doesn't prove anything.'

'Just let Jerry make the dressing if he wants to,' said their father. 'Now, who'd like to see my new placard?' He held up a board on which he had painted the slogan **MAKE LOVE NOT WAR.** 'You two would do well to take my advice,' he laughed.

'You're disgusting!' said Tom, returning his attention to his brother's dressing. 'If you use olive oil I won't eat it!'

'Then don't,' said Jerry. 'It's my recipe. I can do what I like with it.'

'And this is my boot,' sneered Tom, swinging it at Jerry's bottom, 'I can do what I like with it too!' Only he missed and kicked a hole through the 'O' of 'LOVE'. Their father turned the colour of a volcano.

'OUT!' he boomed. And for once his sons did as they were told, rushing to the bottom of the garden and hiding in the bushes in case he tried to beat them with his peace placard.

* * *

While the two brothers were jostling for the most comfortable position in the flowerbed, Jerry put his hand on something strange. It was the size of a golf ball, but the shape of a mushroom. When it twitched Jerry pulled his hand away with a stifled scream.

'What is it?' he cried.

'Mine!' declared Tom, shoving his brother out of the way so that he could pick it up. 'I saw it first.'

'*I* saw it first!' protested Jerry, butting Tom's stomach with his shoulder. The two boys tumbled out of the flowerbed and sprawled across the grass. Jerry was the first to his feet and tried to snatch the mushroom out of Tom's hand, but it held fast.

'Ow!' screamed Tom. 'You're pulling off my skin!' The boys stopped fighting immediately and stared in horror at this peculiar fungus. It had changed colour. It was now fluorescent green, and black roots like the tentacles of a dead jellyfish had grown out of the stalk and buried themselves in Tom's hand.

'What's it doing?' asked Jerry.

'It's sucking my blood,'

shrieked Tom. He tried to punch it off his hand but it was too firmly anchored.

'Is it a leech?' Jerry asked. 'Shall I get a saw and cut it off?'

'Yes,' yelled Tom. 'No! There's no time. Pull it off! Quick!' He sounded so scared all of a sudden that Jerry did as he was told. What surprised them both was the ease with which the black mushroom came away. Now that it was no longer attached to Tom's hand it had lost its green glow.

'It must have finished feeding,' Tom said matter-of-factly.

At the mention of 'feeding', Jerry opened his fingers to drop the mushroom on the ground, but it didn't fall. Its roots were now hooked into *Jerry's* hand and were drawing something warm down the veins in his arm. He flapped his hand above his head.

'Get it off me!' he shouted. 'Get it off!' Tom grabbed a plant plot and smashed it down on the glowing parasite. But even as it fell onto the grass, Tom gasped.

'Look at that,' he said. 'It's grown.' The mushroom was now the size of a grapefruit.

The wrinkles on its black skin had stretched tight. The brothers kicked it into the greenhouse, locked the door so that it couldn't escape and peered at it through the glass. They could have sworn it was breathing.

* * *

That night, neither boy could sleep. Jerry lay on his back in the bottom bunk and kicked the underside of his brother's mattress.

'If you don't stop doing that,' threatened Tom, hurling his pillow into Jerry's face, 'I'll come down there and break your legs.'

'What if it can climb stairs?' whispered Jerry.

'It's a mushroom,' said Tom, 'not a goat.'

'Yes, but what if it's grown again? Did you lock the door?'

'You're scared,' mocked Tom.

'Aren't you?' said Jerry. 'It's like Mum said. Our bad energy's got to go somewhere. What if it's living in that mushroom?'

Tom laughed scornfully. 'How did it get there then?'

'That's obvious. It *sucked* it out.'

'You mean you think it's living off us?'

'Maybe it's a vampire mushroom.'

'Well, it might be living off *me*,' sniggered

Tom, 'because I'm so perfect and taste delicious, but it won't be living off you, because you taste like something a dog parked on the pavement!'

'Shut up!' shouted Jerry, kicking his brother's mattress again. Tom spat on his brother's head then turned over and went to sleep.

* * *

In the greenhouse, the boys' midnight fight caused the mushroom to stir. It wrenched its roots out of the soil, hauled itself up the vertical panes of glass and slipped into the night through a broken window. Minutes later, having dragged itself across the lawn, it flopped through the cat flap like a mutant spider and did what Jerry was afraid of . . . it climbed the stairs. Outside the boys' bedroom it made a noise like smacking lips then squeezed under the door and scuttled, crab-like, towards the snoring. The mushroom was now large enough to stretch its roots between the top and bottom bunks, thus enabling it to sink its teeth into Tom and Jerry simultaneously.

As dawn broke, the mushroom finished feeding. It had grown to over ten times its original size and was so sleepy that it lay down in the corner of the room behind the curtains. During the transfer of nourishment from their arms, Tom and Jerry had not made a sound. Now that the blob was asleep, they started fighting again. They argued so loudly about who had left the door unlocked that their parents rushed in to put a stop to it. Mr Ganglion arrived first with a placard that he had painted specially for the occasion . . .

STOP THE FIGHTING! GO TO SLEEP!

. . . while Mrs Ganglion ranted on about selfishness. She had just reached the bit about 'respecting others' when something behind the curtain caught her eye.

'Have you got a cat in this room?' she asked, mistaking one of the fungus's roots for a tail.

'No,' said Jerry. 'It's a mushroom.'

Tom punched the top of his arm. 'That is so typical of you!' he moaned. 'You can never keep a secret.'

'What is it?' snapped their mother.

'Like Jerry the Snitch said,' said Tom. 'It's a mushroom we found in the garden. Only it's not really a mushroom, because it sticks its roots in our arms and sucks all this stuff out.' Mrs Ganglion marched over to the window, drew the curtain and screamed. 'It's grown again!' Tom noted. 'When we found it, it fitted in the palm of my hand. Now look. Two feeds and it's . . . big.' It was size of a black bin bag and its tentacles writhed like Medusa's snakes.

'Good God!' whispered the boys' mother fearfully. 'You remember that bad energy I said had infected this house . . . I think we've just found it!'

Quick, aren't they, the Ganglions?

The alien mushroom was content to lie behind the curtain until the brothers had another fight. Then it slid its roots across the floor, plugged them into the boys' wrists and drank till it was green. Mr and Mrs Ganglion ordered the boys to stop arguing until they had found out what this thing was, but their pleas fell on deaf ears. Tom and Jerry argued over who had found the thing in the first place, over who had more food in their arm, over which of them the mushroom thought was tastier . . . in fact, they argued over everything to do with this alien being without once making the connection that something born of evil was more than likely to be evil itself!

You should meet my mother!

While Mr Ganglion designed a placard to counter the alien threat in the bedroom – **MAKE MUSHROOM OMELETTES NOT WAR!** – Mrs Ganglion sought help from scientists to discover what this creature was. They all agreed that it was fed and kept alive by badness, but nobody could explain what it was, until the family doctor made a home visit to treat Mrs Ganglion's shredded nerves, and said casually, 'That thing in the corner? That's a wart.'

It was worse than that. On closer inspection, government health officials said it was a *Nuclear* Wart. Theoretical physicists explained that a Nuclear Wart expanding exponentially was capable of destroying the planet in less time than it takes to eat a Dodo. The media circus that suddenly appeared on the Ganglion's doorstep only served to feed the wart's growth by pitting Tom against Jerry. Journalists wanted to know which of the brothers was the baddest and therefore the provider of the most food for the wart, and the two of them were happy to argue the point in print, on the radio and even on television, where they had a massive brawl on *Jeremy Bile's Early Morning Punch-up Show* and knocked each others' teeth out.

Tom and Jerry were tagged the Bad Boys of Riddlesden Knob. Within a week of the media getting hold of the story the Nuclear Wart was big enough to anchor its roots in the garden and hover over the house like a black Zeppelin. The prime minister ordered the army to attack it with wart-shrivelling liquid, but his grasp of military tactics was frankly feeble and the liquid simply splashed off the wart's skin. In desperation, several witches were contacted for their ancient wart remedies, which was why the Ganglions had thirty-two kilos of raw lamb's liver buried in their back garden. But superstitious nonsense was no match for this Nuclear Wart either.

* * *

As the world was rapidly coming to realise, a Nuclear Wart, once started, is virtually impossible to stop.

Then, one Tuesday, having just had a bust up on the Radio One *Breakfast Show*, Tom and Jerry were being driven home when they saw something that briefly checked their tongues. The wart had detached itself from their house and had risen into the sky. With thousands of long, black roots dangling beneath it, it looked exactly like the mushroom cloud that follows the explosion of a nuclear bomb.

Mr Ganglion was protesting on the front lawn with a **STOP THE WART!** placard when Jerry jumped out of the chauffeur-driven car.

'What's happening?' he asked.

'It just took off,' said his mother. 'Maybe it doesn't need you two anymore. You gave birth to it, but now it's all grown up and can find food for itself.' The Nuclear Wart had stopped over a maximum security prison. Its roots squirmed across the flat roof and slithered into the cells. After ten minutes of refuelling it was on its way again, only now it was twice the size.

* * *

While the Nuclear Wart had been living with Tom and Jerry its size had been controllable. There was only so much evil it could extract from their arms. But now that it was free to mine badness wherever it found it – in newspaper offices, in football crowds, in the Houses of Parliament – it grew at a terrifying rate. Like a thick black cloud swaddling the sky, the Nuclear Wart brought darkness to the earth.

'Is this the end of the world?' whispered Jerry.

'Don't be stupid,' said his father. 'While we've still got my peace placards there's always hope that the human race will come together in opposition to the wart!'

'But it's getting bigger by the day,' said Tom. 'Scientists say that by tomorrow it will be bigger than the earth.'

'Still, let's look on the bright side,' said Mrs Ganglion. 'At least you two have stopped arguing. You haven't hit each other in a week.'

'There doesn't seem much point anymore,' said Jerry. 'It seems rather selfish that a silly little dispute over oil should lead to this Nuclear Wart.'

'It *was* silly, wasn't it?' conceded Tom. 'And I'm very sorry.'

'Me too,' said his brother. 'I wish

someone would invent a time machine so that we could go back to a time *before* wart and undo all the fighting that we did.' Tom agreed.

* * *

Unfortunately, the boys' remorse came far too late. The following morning the Nuclear Wart surrounded the Earth in evil. Like the Mothership of an alien attack force, the Motherwart blocked out the sun and starved the planet of heat, until every human being emerged from their dwelling to see what was happening. Then it struck. The warthead split apart revealing billions of spiked black roots that exploded from its belly towards the ground. They pierced human skulls like arrows and tore through flesh and bone until they reached their hearts. Then they extracted the badness, threw away the human shell and plunged on further, through the Earth's crust, through layers of molten rock, down into the Earth's core, where the Nuclear Wart sucked the life out of the planet, until all that was left was a frazzled black mass spinning through space and trailing smoke like a burnt Yorkshire Pudding.

It's true what they say; Wart *is* hell.

Actually. it's a wart in the park compared to the fun and games I put you through down here in The Darkness! I know what you're thinking . . . You're thinking. 'I'm not scared of that Night-night Porter anymore. Now that Earth has gone the Hothell Darkness must have gone too! Hurrah! I shan't be going down there after all to be tortured!' I've got news for you. This hothell is so deep in the bowels of the earth it's like living in a nuclear bunker. Nothing gets through. not even a wart's roots. So everything's carrying on as normal despite the fact that the whole planet's dead and has got a new name.

You haven't heard? It's taken Mars by storm. As part of their Saturday night entertainment Martians have been watching the annihilation of the human race on their tellys. There've got a reality TV show up there called 'I'm A Celebrity Get Me Off This Planet Before A Wart Sucks The Life Out Of It' in which celebrities are plucked from planets just before a wart sucks the life out of them and flown to Mars for a party with balloons and champagne where the viewers have to come up with a name for the dead planet before the celebrity is dropped through the floor into a cage with sixteen Martian Hellhounds, who tear him limb from limb in a frenzied attack of unimaginable pointlessness. Sounds really good, doesn't it? Anyway, the new name the Martian viewers came up with for Earth wasn't Weart or Warth as you might expect, but Verrucca. It's clever. For what is a Verrucca if not an upside down wart in disguise? And was this not the biggest wart in de skies that the universe had ever seen?

I think it was.

Would you mind awfully if I got personal for a moment? I know I can. You've spent so long reading this book of Grizzly Tales that I feel I know you like a blubber. And because we're so close I can tell you what I'm feeling in my heart. All this talk of blubbers and sicksters has made me realise how lonely I am in this hothell. Yes, I get to stake out bad babies for the birds and feed the eels with guests who turn up late for breakfast. So what? Most of the time I'm tramping the corridors looking for friends with a bucket of chocolate ants in one hand and a funnel for force feeding geese in the other . . . when do I ever get any time for fun? If you'd just say 'YES' and sign the Release Form below we can seal our bond in blood. I'll get the spigot installed in your artery before you can shout 'Vampires at Twelve O'Clock!' and we can become Blood Blubbers. Then we can do everything together. I can punch your head and force you to give me your flapjacks. I can break your toys and tell your friends that you're a crybaby. I can smash car windows and blame it on you. I can even steal your clothes and tell your mum that you hit me. What do you say? Isn't that what Blood Blubbers are for?

RELEASE FORM
<u>This is a Get Out Of Jail Free Card</u>

I hereby release the Night-night Porter from prison for stealing all my blood and turning me into a dried-out husk, like one of those salted fish you can buy in Caribbean Markets (if you don't know what I mean, Google 'Salt Fish' and have a look at the pictures) under the pretence of wanting to become my Blood Blubber.

Signed..

Where are you going?
Come back. I've got the spigot ready.